THE HUNGER GAMES: CATCHING FIRE

THE OFFICIAL ILLUSTRATED MOVIE COMPANION

by Kate Egan

ACKNOWLEDGMENTS

Thank you to the cast and crew of *The Hunger Games: Catching Fire* for generously sharing your experiences.

Thank you to Francis Lawrence, Nina Jacobson, and Jon Kilik for giving the fans a truly informative and entertaining peek behind the scenes.

Thank you to Paula Kupfer, Edwina Cumberbatch, and Amanda Maes for all of your help. And to the rest of the great team at Lionsgate: Tim Palen, Erik Feig, Julie Fontaine, Jennifer Peterson, Danielle DePalma, Douglas Lloyd, John Fu, and Erika Schimik.

Thank you to the talented and dedicated team at Scholastic: Ellie Berger, Rachel Coun, Rick DeMonico, David Levithan, and Lindsay Walter. To Emily Seife, I am so grateful to you for asking all of the right questions and keeping everything moving along smoothly.

And thank you to Suzanne Collins: As always, it was a joy to work with you.

—K.E.

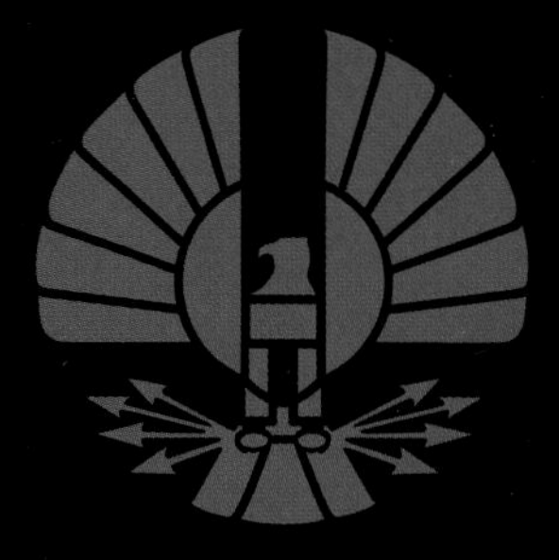

Front cover photography by Tim Palen

Unit Still Photography by Murray Close

The Hunger Games world premiere (pages 6-7, 8 bottom, 9 top and bottom): Eric Charbonneau

Photo of Suzanne Collins (page 8 top right): Alberto E. Rodriguez/Getty Images

Entertainment Weekly covers (page 10 bottom left and right): Entertainment Weekly® used by permission of Entertainment Weekly, Inc.

The Hunger Games publicity tour (page 11 top): courtesy of Lions Gate

Dresses from *La Glacon* collection (page 124 bottom left and right): Ulet Ifansasti/Getty Images Entertainment

Yugoslav sculptures (page 89 left and right): Jan Kempenaers @ KASK School of Arts, Ghent

Published by Scholastic Press, an imprint of Scholastic Inc., *Publishers since 1920.* Scholastic, Scholastic Press, and associated logos are trademarks and/or registered trademarks of Scholastic Inc.

Library of Congress Control Number: 2013946783

ISBN 978-0-545-59933-7

12 10 9 8 7 6 5 4 3 2 1   13 14 15 16 17 18 19/0

Printed in the U.S.A. 40

First edition, November 2013

This book was designed by Rick DeMonico and Heather Barber

CONTENTS

PART 1
THE HUNGER GAMES CATCHES FIRE
4

PART 2
MOVING FORWARD
18

PART 3
EXPANDING THE WORLD OF PANEM
48

PART 4
DESIGNING THE ARENA
84

PART 5
CREATING COSTUMES, DESIGNING FACES
116

PART 6
LOOKING AHEAD
152

PART 1

THE HUNGER GAMES CATCHES FIRE

THE WORLD WILL BE WATCHING

On March 23, 2012, the world was watching.

Across the country, theaters were sold out. Fans grasped their tickets, waiting to take their seats.

At the stroke of midnight, *The Hunger Games* — the most highly anticipated film of the year — exploded into theaters.

Like the book it was based on, the movie was an instant sensation. A phenomenon. A force. Viewers connected with the characters, the themes, and the story in a visceral and powerful way.

For more than a year, fans had been tantalized by news about the movie. Initial announcements about casting and production were followed first

> ***May the odds be ever in your favor.***
> ***— The Hunger Games***

by a sneak peek, which debuted at the MTV Video Music Awards in August, and then by the release of the full trailer in November. In January, fans could hear the haunting melody of Taylor Swift's "Safe & Sound" on the radio. Now, at last, audiences would be able to see how the rest of the film had come together.

The night before the March 12 world premiere, hard-core fans gathered at fan headquarters, called the Hob, in downtown Los Angeles. The first 400 to arrive would receive wristbands granting entry to the star-studded event. For these *Hunger Games* devotees, sleeping outside on the city's streets was a small price to pay for the chance to be among the first to see the film on the big screen.

The next day, throngs of people crowded near the theater, waiting for a glimpse of the stars. The flashes of hundreds of cameras filled the cool evening with light. A million more viewers watched the

ACTORS JOSH HUTCHERSON AND JENNIFER LAWRENCE POSE FOR THE CAMERAS AND THE FANS AT THE 2012 *HUNGER GAMES* MOVIE WORLD PREMIERE IN LOS ANGELES.

live streaming video online. The excitement built as the limos began to arrive.

The crowd roared when it spotted Josh Hutcherson, who played Peeta Mellark, and Liam Hemsworth, who played Gale Hawthorne. It welcomed the as-yet-unknown actors who played the young tributes; the major stars like Woody Harrelson, Elizabeth Banks, Stanley Tucci, and Donald Sutherland; and Suzanne Collins, the author of the bestselling *Hunger Games* novels. Many of them walked into the crowd, signing books and posters with a smile. In return, fans expressed their excitement by giving the actors the famous District 12 salute.

Finally, Jennifer Lawrence stepped out onto the black carpet, and the crowd went crazy! It was as if Katniss Everdeen was walking through the streets of the Capitol.

SUZANNE COLLINS, AUTHOR OF THE BESTSELLING *HUNGER GAMES* SERIES, AT THE *HUNGER GAMES* WORLD PREMIERE.

THE CROWD GATHERS AT THE NOKIA THEATRE FOR THE MOVIE'S MARCH 12 WORLD PREMIERE.

Jennifer Lawrence, wearing a gold gown by Prabal Gurung, pauses in the spotlight on the black carpet at *The Hunger Games*'s world premiere.

Actor Liam Hemsworth signs books for excited fans.

A PHENOMENON

The Hunger Games was a massive hit. For four weeks, it was the most popular movie in the nation, eventually grossing $408 million in the United States alone. It was the biggest-ever release in the month of March, the third-highest-grossing film of 2012, and the thirteenth-highest-grossing film of all time.

Like the audiences, critics loved it. *Entertainment Weekly* called it "a muscular, honorable, unflinching translation of Collins' vision," and *Rolling Stone* said, "My advice is to keep your eyes on Lawrence, who turns the movie into a victory by presenting a heroine propelled by principle."

The movie was on a slew of magazine covers and everywhere online. The stars' publicity tour, in malls across America, averaged more than 8,000 fans at each stop. Sales of *The Hunger Games* merchandise — from mockingjay pins to replicas of Katniss's bow — were off the charts. The movie's soundtrack — featuring artists like Arcade Fire and Maroon 5 — debuted at number one and earned two Grammy nominations. Sales of the original books were through the roof.

Erik Feig, President of Production of the Lionsgate Motion Picture Group, feels sure that audiences connected to the movie because they connected so strongly to the character of Katniss. "The first movie did a

TOP: THE OFFICIAL POSTER FOR THE FIRST *THE HUNGER GAMES* FILM
BOTTOM: *THE HUNGER GAMES* ACTORS AND IMAGES WERE PROMINENTLY FEATURED ON MAGAZINES IN THE MONTHS LEADING UP TO THE FILM.
OPPOSITE: A MOCKINGJAY PIN

The Hunger Games's publicity tour brought the actors to fans at locations across the country — including this one, the Mall of America in Bloomington, Minnesota.

great job of getting into Katniss's head," he says. "Just as the reader sees the world from her perspective in the books, every step of the way in the film you really feel what it's like to be Katniss. *The Hunger Games* feels real because it is emotionally real."

The Hunger Games was bigger than any pop chart or bestseller list. It was a movie that crossed boundaries. A movie that spoke to people. A movie that became a cultural sensation. Everyone was talking about it, from teens to their parents and grandparents.

What had begun as a young adult series was now the subject of speeches and sermons, required reading in book clubs and English classes. Suddenly, archery was a popular sport, gyms were offering fitness classes inspired by tributes' training, and *Katniss* and *Rue* were popular names for babies.

On one level, the movie was an edge-of-your-seat adventure, in which Katniss fought to be the last tribute left standing. But *The Hunger Games* spoke to audiences on a higher level, too, asking probing questions about how our culture exploits its stars and heroes. It looked candidly at our interest in violence, and challenged audiences to find the limits of that interest. It offered the image of a girl, still untainted by the culture of the Capitol, capturing its attention and daring to defy it.

With its unforgettable characters and powerful questions, *The Hunger Games* resonated — and continues to resonate — far beyond teen audiences, becoming an instant classic across the globe.

The Hunger Games was only the beginning, however. In the next film in the series, *The Hunger Games: Catching Fire*, the stakes would be even higher.

VICTORY TOUR

WITH KATNISS EVERDEEN AND PEETA MELLARK
WINNERS OF THE 74TH HUNGER GAMES

FB.COM/THECAPITOLPN IMAX LIONSGATE

In the lead-up to *The Hunger Games: Catching Fire*, Lionsgate Studio created Victory Tour posters.

THE STORY CONTINUES

The Hunger Games caught fire with the story of an extraordinary girl facing down a cruel regime and its terrible Hunger Games. Viewers were captivated by Katniss's fierce loyalty to her family, her courage and resourcefulness in the Games, and her eventual refusal to play by the rules.

The next film, *The Hunger Games: Catching Fire*, meets up with Katniss several months later, when her single act of rebellion has ignited a storm that she never intended. Author Suzanne Collins describes Katniss's state of mind at the start of the film: "Katniss is now a veteran of the arena, suffering from post-traumatic stress disorder, and trying to manage the psychological wounds she received in the first Games. Both the terror of being hunted and the taking of other tributes' lives haunt her. It's impossible for her to get any distance from the experience because from the opening she's forced to go on the Victory Tour, one district at a time, and pretend to be honoring the Games while she's faced with the families of the dead children. What she's experienced affects choices she makes about when and how to engage the Capitol and, in particular, President Snow."

The movie begins with a surprise visitor at Katniss's new home in the Victor's Village. It's the president of Panem, Coriolanus Snow, with a chilling message for her. He doesn't believe — not for one minute — the star-crossed lovers act she pulled off in the arena with fellow tribute Peeta Mellark. But her life and future will depend on convincing everybody else in the country that it was for real. Otherwise, there is no way to explain how Katniss forced the Capitol Gamemakers to bend their rules for her — and no way to stop the revolutionary wave set off by her defiance.

With Snow's words echoing in her mind, Katniss and Peeta embark on the cross-country Victory Tour that comes after winning the Games. She does her best to convince the people of Panem that she's just a girl in love, and that the only thought on her mind are plans for her upcoming marriage to Peeta. But there is growing unrest in Panem. And even if the crowds believe Katniss, President Snow does not. When she returns from the tour, Katniss discovers that her district has brutal new Peacekeepers, and vicious punishment for those who disobey them. Like her.

Then, for the seventy-fifth anniversary of the rebellion, the country's laws demand a special edition of the Hunger Games. It's called a Quarter Quell, and it happens once every twenty-five years: a set of Games with different rules. This year, for the third-ever Quell, Snow decrees the tributes will be selected from the pool of victors from former games — one man, one woman, from each district.

MRS. EVERDEEN (PAULA MALCOMSON) AND PRIMROSE EVERDEEN (WILLOW SHIELDS)

As the only living female victor from District 12, Katniss is going back into the arena. It's like the nightmares that have interrupted her sleep ever since she returned from the Hunger Games, only this time it's for real. The president will make sure she never comes back, Katniss knows. But maybe she can save Peeta, and at last repay all she feels she owes him.

So they go back to the Capitol with great fanfare. They meet the other tributes and begin to train. The victors are different from the tributes the

"In *Catching Fire*, the story evolves from a gladiator game to a rebellion." — Suzanne Collins

last time around, hardened and bitter, even though they're the Capitol's "winners." Katniss's only goal is to seek out anyone who might help keep Peeta alive.

She thinks she is building alliances. But Katniss slowly sees that another alliance has developed among the victors, one that doesn't include her. And it's not until the end of the Quarter Quell that she discovers the shocking truth about its purpose.

"In *Catching Fire*, the story evolves from a gladiator game to a rebellion," Suzanne Collins explains. "The Hunger Games, which have always been a symbol of the Capitol's power over the districts, now become the focal point for political dissent. Since the Games are televised, they become a rare opportunity for the rebels to communicate to all the people in the districts. The stakes aren't just personal, they're national. The outcome changes the course of history for Panem."

Somehow, Katniss must find a place in this highly charged political moment. Director Francis Lawrence — no relation to the actress playing Katniss — says, "Katniss Everdeen has no interest in

PEETA MELLARK (JOSH HUTCHERSON), EFFIE TRINKET (ELIZABETH BANKS), AND KATNISS EVERDEEN (JENNIFER LAWRENCE) DURING THE DISTRICT 12 REAPING FOR THE QUARTER QUELL.

Peeta (Josh Hutcherson) and Katniss (Jennifer Lawrence) stand together during the Victory Tour.

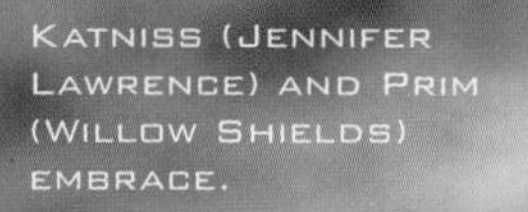

KATNISS (JENNIFER LAWRENCE) AND PRIM (WILLOW SHIELDS) EMBRACE.

being a hero. We can really relate to the way that she has these very personal needs and wants: to protect herself, to protect the people she loves. Now new things are being asked of her, and she doesn't want any part of them. She doesn't want to be responsible for all these people. She doesn't want anyone looking up to her. She has enough to worry about on her own. It's one of the things that's the most believable about her as a character. But eventually she will have to make some hard choices."

Producer Nina Jacobson elaborates: "Katniss has been awakened, but she is not yet ready to lead. She's still asking questions. Why did she save Peeta? Was it to win the Games? Was it to save herself? Was it an ethical stand? Or does she really love him? Katniss has to start to answer these questions as she sees increasing evidence of the way she's inspired the people of the districts, the way they are looking to her for leadership. She doesn't yet see herself as that leader, but she is slowly growing into the role."

Like Katniss in the arena, *The Hunger Games* movie became more than anyone dared to dream it could be. The spectacular success of the film would give Lionsgate, the movie studio, the ability to assemble another top-notch team for bringing the next part of Suzanne Collins's epic story to the screen.

"*Catching Fire* opens up the story that was begun in *The Hunger Games* and shows a broader scope of the world. At the same time, now we know these characters and love these characters, and can push forward into their stories in a very emotional way."

— Francis Lawrence

PART 2
MOVING FORWARD

Director Francis Lawrence on set.

THE FIRST STEP

The film's creators were excited about the new opportunities awaiting them as they looked ahead to making the sequel to *The Hunger Games*. With one hit movie behind her, producer Nina Jacobson knew there would be a hungry audience for *The Hunger Games: Catching Fire*. Viewers would have high hopes and huge expectations for the new movie, and it was up to her team to deliver something fans would love just as much.

"We needed to communicate to ourselves and to the fans that we were still aiming every bit as high, that we would still be every bit as ambitious with subsequent movies," Jacobson says. "We would still take creative risks and still honor the books the way we'd honored the first one."

"The right director was one who'd have a high level of emotional acuity, in order to tell Katniss's story and show the psychological trauma she has experienced, while at the same time being a gifted visual stylist." — Erik Feig

Fortunately, Lionsgate found exactly the right director for the second film, someone who was ready to take on this important job. Lionsgate's Erik Feig remembers just what he was looking for: "The right director was one who'd have a high level of emotional acuity, in order to tell Katniss's story and show the psychological trauma she has experienced, while at the same time being a gifted visual stylist who could do justice to the bigger scope and world of *The Hunger Games: Catching Fire*." Enter Francis Lawrence.

DIRECTOR FRANCIS LAWRENCE CHATS WITH JENNIFER LAWRENCE (KATNISS) AND LIAM HEMSWORTH (GALE) ON SET IN DISTRICT 12.

Lawrence is known for his crisp visual style and his rich imagination. He began his career as a successful director of music videos and commercials, eventually finding his way to feature films. He was the director of the blockbuster *I Am Legend*, starring Will Smith, as well as *Water for Elephants*, another movie based on a bestselling book. Lawrence had plenty of experience creating futuristic worlds, directing heart-stopping action, and kindling romance against unlikely backdrops . . . all of which he would draw on for his new project.

Lawrence was eager to direct the second film in the series. "Part of the fun of making the movie that follows *The Hunger Games* is that the story opens up in all kinds of different ways. I loved the idea of helping to craft the characters, letting them grow, and creating new scenes with them where they're digging into even meatier stuff than they had in the first film," he says.

He looked forward to entering and expanding the world of the first *Hunger Games* film. The new movie would feature much more of Panem, as Katniss and Peeta would visit the districts on the Victory Tour, and also show even more of the Capitol. Plus there was a whole new arena to create. Lawrence was excited and inspired by all of these opportunities.

In the first movie, the tributes are out to kill one another, and the main action in the arena consists of hand-to-hand conflict between them.

Director Francis Lawrence works with Sam Claflin (Finnick), Josh Hutcherson (Peeta), and Jennifer Lawrence (Katniss) on set for an arena scene in Hawaii.

In the second movie, however, the Games are different. The tributes are past victors who have discovered that winning the Games isn't all it's cracked up to be, and who are shocked to be thrown back into the arena. As a result, the violence comes less from tributes attacking tributes than from the arena attacking all of them.

"I wanted to make the book, not to reinvent it."
— Francis Lawrence

Lawrence saw the obstacles of the arena as a dual challenge to him as a filmmaker: to create amazing action sequences while at the same time creating a range of emotions in the viewer. "I find that part of the fun of any set piece or action piece is that it feels emotionally different from another one," he explains. "The fog, for me, is actually a sequence about sacrifice and loss; the monkey attack is about fear, and so forth."

Lawrence worked with author Suzanne Collins, as well as screenwriters Simon Beaufoy and Michael deBruyn, to draft a screenplay that remained true to the original novel while also maximizing its dramatic potential. "I wanted to make the book, not to reinvent it," says Lawrence. "It became this really great, organic group of people working together to best tell this story on film."

District 12 Mentor Haymitch Abernathy, played by Woody Harrelson.

ASSEMBLING A CAST

In *The Hunger Games: Catching Fire*, new actors would join the core group of talent that included Academy Award™–winner Jennifer Lawrence, Josh Hutcherson, Liam Hemsworth, Woody Harrelson, Elizabeth Banks, Lenny Kravitz, and Donald Sutherland. The biggest roles to fill would be those of Plutarch Heavensbee, the new Head Gamemaker, and the two victors Katniss comes to know best: Finnick Odair and Johanna Mason. "There's action in the movie," says producer

"Finnick is very confident and charming. He's that face that everybody knows. . . . But he's not able to share his feelings, ever, because he feels that eyes are always on him. He's not who he seems to be."
— Sam Claflin

CASTING AROUND THE WORLD

The process of casting is one that can span continents. Erik Feig describes the initial stages of casting the role of Finnick: "Casting directors from all over the world post video auditions of their actors reading the role on a special site just for the filmmakers. We saw every kind of actor that you can imagine, from the US, the UK, Australia. . . ." It was when they found Sam Claflin that everything clicked. Feig continues, "The first time we saw Sam's audition on the site, the volume happened to be on mute — but even without any sound, he just popped off the screen. He brought that kind of presence to Finnick, that vulnerability that makes us understand and care what Finnick is all about. Then when we actually turned on the sound and got to hear how he was saying it and the intelligence that came through, we knew one hundred percent that we wanted this actor."

Jon Kilik, "but it's really character driven, so you've got to have great actors who can bring multiple dimensions to each part."

The first actor cast was Jeffrey Wright as Beetee, with whom Jon Kilik had worked on four previous films. "He's an actor who can morph into almost any role," Kilik says. "He's versatile and extremely talented. This part requires someone who could be at once smart and methodical and a little bit dangerous. There was no doubt that Jeffrey would be able to carry it off." Wright's past movies include *Casino Royale*, *Basquiat*, *Broken Flowers*, and *W.* In *The Hunger Games: Catching Fire*, he would play a victor with sophisticated technical skills and an early recognition of Katniss's power.

For Finnick, Francis Lawrence and the producers were looking for an actor with the proper balance of swagger and sensitivity. British actor Sam Claflin, best known for his role as William in *Snow White and the Huntsman*, was perfect for the part. Claflin explains: "Finnick is very confident and charming. He's that face that everybody knows. Every man wants to be him, and every woman wants to be with him. But he's not able to share his feelings, ever, because he feels that eyes are always on him. He's not who he seems to be."

At his audition and throughout shooting, Claflin was able to portray both sides of this complicated character. He was even game for the infamous sugar-cube scene, where he meets Katniss for the first time. "I don't think she's ever met anybody like him," says Jennifer Lawrence. "Finnick hides his true self, and it takes Katniss a while to see what he is covering up."

In future movies, Finnick's role will evolve, and the team felt that Claflin was up to that challenge, too.

JEFFREY WRIGHT AS THE QUIRKY BUT BRILLIANT DISTRICT 3 VICTOR BEETEE.

Peeta (Josh Hutcherson), Katniss (Jennifer Lawrence), and Haymitch (Woody Harrelson) come to terms with the reality of the Victory Tour.

The ever-charming Finnick Odair (Sam Claflin) approaches Katniss (Jennifer Lawrence) in the Training Center.

"Finnick is really three different characters over the course of the series," says Lionsgate's Erik Feig. "Katniss's first impression is that he's the Capitol's peacock, and that's what we see in the first scene where we meet him. In the arena, he becomes a different kind of Finnick, an ally and a friend. And of course he becomes a third kind of Finnick as we move into *Mockingjay*. So that takes a complicated, sophisticated actor, someone who can balance Finnick's arrogance and cockiness with likability, someone who can show

TAKING FLIGHT

Bruno Gunn was cast in the role of Brutus, one of the Careers from District 2. "I was on my way to Rome to visit family, but I had to stop in Toronto," he remembers. "I've got maybe less than an hour to catch my flight, and I'm hauling to the gate, when my phone rings. It's my manager, and she says, 'You're Brutus.' And I say, 'You're joking, right? Is this for real?' So then I get on a plane, a nine-hour flight, and I can't even call anyone. And wouldn't you know . . . there are six movies to choose from on the plane. And everyone is watching *The Hunger Games*!"

District 7 victor Johanna Mason, played by Jena Malone, refreshes her weaponry skills in the Training Center.

what his life has cost him."

Katniss doesn't know it yet, but her future depends on Finnick and on Johanna Mason, a prickly female victor. "When it came time to find our Johanna," Nina Jacobson remembers, "we really had no choice but to cast Jena Malone. When she came in, her audition was so intense and raw and dangerous — she just nailed it." Malone had been a child actress and was making her way into ever-more-demanding roles, including a stint in *Doubt* on Broadway. "She did a scene from the book," says Jacobson, "where she volunteers to go into the woods after both Finnick and Katniss have been traumatized by jabberjays among the trees. And she basically says, 'I'm not like you. There's no one left I love.' And the way she said this line, you felt that it wasn't self-pitying, it was just this devastating statement that she was alone in the world and that she drew her courage from having no one to lose."

> **"When [Jena Malone] came in, her audition was so intense and raw and dangerous — she just nailed it."**
> **— Nina Jacobson**

Malone had first learned of the *Hunger Games* books from her younger sister, an avid reader. "Her whole face changed when she told me about the

REBELLION THROUGH FASHION

As Katniss's stylist, Cinna, Lenny Kravitz plays a crucial role in *The Hunger Games: Catching Fire*. Kravitz says of his character, "He's showing his rebellious side, but instead of being loud about it, he's using it in his work, in his creations. President Snow wants Katniss to have a wedding, so Cinna designs an extravagant dress. But then the dress turns into something else entirely: a mockingjay, the symbol of rebellion. Nobody expects it from Cinna, but he definitely has his say." In the Capitol, Cinna is the only person Katniss feels she can trust, and the bond between the two characters grows and deepens in *The Hunger Games: Catching Fire*. Cinna's loyalty gives Katniss courage and, of course, an unforgettable style.

Johanna Mason (Jena Malone) surveys the arena.

books," Malone explains. "And I thought, *Wow, this must be something pretty interesting.*" Like many of the new cast members, she already felt connected to the series, and thrilled to be a part of a film that would reach such a huge audience.

For Plutarch, the team dreamed of casting Philip Seymour Hoffman. "We wanted Plutarch to be scheming and brilliant and masterful and conniving, and we knew that Hoffman could deliver on all fronts," says Erik Feig. The producers and Francis Lawrence went to see him in his Broadway production of *Death of a Salesman* — and what they saw convinced them he was the man for the job. They waited patiently with fingers crossed until he had the time to read the script and decide whether he wanted to sign on. When he did, they were ecstatic. Audiences would know Hoffman from his Academy Award™–winning performance in *Capote*, as well as his star turns in movies like *Moneyball* and *The Master*.

Coproducer Bryan Unkeless says, "Philip Seymour Hoffman brings substance to the role of Plutarch — he has experience, intelligence, and depth.

HEAD GAMEMAKER PLUTARCH HEAVENSBEE (PHILIP SEYMOUR HOFFMAN)

President Snow, played by returning actor Donald Sutherland, meets with head Gamemaker Plutarch Heavensbee (Philip Seymour Hoffman).

With him in the role, you can see how President Snow would work with someone like him. You can see that Snow would respect and understand him, even follow his advice." Unkeless adds, "Plutarch also has a unique understanding of the way in which entertainment can be used to manipulate the masses; he is a master at propaganda."

Director Francis Lawrence worked closely with Hoffman to craft his relationship with President Snow. Many of the scenes the two characters have together are not drawn from the book, but were developed by the actors and director. "A few of his big key moments were completely new creations for us," Lawrence says. "At first no one is quite sure why Plutarch Heavensbee, a retired Gamemaker, would come volunteer to take over this Quarter Quell for Snow. Eventually we learn that he is trying to figure out how to get rid of Katniss in the

"Philip Seymour Hoffman brings substance to the role of Plutarch — he has experience, intelligence, and depth." — Bryan Unkeless

"I've been acting for fifty years, and I thought I'd reached a point where I wouldn't be wearing a black-and-silver jumpsuit. But here I am!"
— Lynn Cohen

smartest way possible. Then, toward the end of the film, we discover another facet of Plutarch's plans."

Even before she knew what *The Hunger Games* was, people were telling Lynn Cohen, a longtime character actress, that she needed to be in the movie. Cohen recalls, "Months ago, a friend called and said, 'You know, you should be playing Mags.' So I put down my phone and called my agent and I said, 'I don't know . . . there's something called Mags that somebody said I'm right for.' So he said something like, 'Okay, um. I'll take care of it. . . .' Then I'm in Tuscany about two months after that, and my granddaughter's reading the third part of the *Hunger Games*, and she says 'Hey, Grandma? You know what? You should be doing Mags.'" Cohen adds, "I've been acting for fifty years, and I thought I'd reached a point where I wouldn't be wearing a black-and-silver jumpsuit. But here I am!"

LYNN COHEN PLAYS MAGS, A VICTOR FROM DISTRICT 4.

Across the board, the new actors were overjoyed to be joining the cast, knowing they would be working with a top-of-the-line team on a movie that spoke to viewers around the world.

THE ROLE OF MENTOR

Woody Harrelson's character, mentor Haymitch Abernathy, is unpredictable and out of control. While Haymitch and Peeta manage to get along, he and Katniss have a contentious relationship. Behind the scenes, though, he is doing all he can to help her. Harrelson says, "We may not see it on-screen, but Haymitch knows this is a pivotal time for Katniss, that she is the symbol of the coming rebellion. He doesn't want anyone to see what he's doing, but he's always on her side."

Johanna Mason (Jena Malone) uses weapons in the Training Center, while District 1 victors Cashmere (Stephanie Leigh Schlund) and Gloss (Alan Ritchson) look on.

GETTING READY

Whether they were new to the cast or not, the actors went through some basic training to prepare for the film, especially the tributes. For them, it was about getting into the sort of shape that would be necessary for them to carry off the action scenes without physical strain.

Stunt coordinator Chad Stahelski met with director Francis Lawrence to discuss what weapons would be available in the Cornucopia. From there, he was able to figure out which skill sets would need to be highlighted in training.

Alan Ritchson, who plays Gloss, says, "We hit the gym with the stunt guys. They taught me how to throw these knives, and all these tuck-and-roll gymnastics and martial arts. It was one of the hardest things I've ever done. I would be completely drenched, completely exhausted, but it was great." Sam Claflin adds, "I learned a new trick every day, trying different flips and what have you. It's like every schoolboy's dream. I love stunt work and getting my hands dirty. This has been my most physical project yet, by a long shot."

Within weeks, the new actors went from learning how to hold their weapons to learning to throw them with confidence. Stephanie Leigh Schlund, who plays Cashmere, a victor from District 1, says she can now handle knives in a "very casual, I've-done-it-all-my-life sort of way," just like a real Career. Jena Malone adds, "Chad is amazing at being able to bring out people's individual strengths. He'll see me playing with a move and say, 'Oh, do that again.' He finds things you are good at and makes you great."

Katniss (Jennifer Lawrence) works on her knot-tying skills in the Training Center.

Meanwhile, returning actors had a strong foundation to build on. Chad Stahelski remembers, "With Katniss, we took her bow-and-arrow training up to the next level. We spent a lot of time with Jen in the gym, doing archery and physical conditioning and hand-to-hand combat." Jennifer Lawrence adds, "I love doing the stunts in this movie. The extra months of training were definitely worth getting to do some of my own."

There was an emotional difference to the training for the second movie, though. "The backstory for each of the characters is a bit darker and more serious," Stahelski explains. "Katniss and Peeta and the other tributes have previous experience — they know what's expected of them, so you can take the action up a notch."

"I love doing the stunts in this movie. The extra months of training were definitely worth getting to do some of my own."
— Jennifer Lawrence

District 2 victor Brutus,
played by Bruno Gunn,
prepares to throw a spear
in the Training Center.

DEFINING NEW CHARACTERS

As they worked to embody their characters physically, the new actors were also digging deep into the identities they would take on in the film.

Like the other newcomers, Jena Malone had to imagine what her character, Johanna Mason, had been through before she arrived in the Capitol for the Quarter Quell. Malone says, "It's not easy to recover from being in the Hunger Games and then deal with the pressure the Capitol puts on a victor to become a puppet. You become a sort of Capitolistic pawn, and you have to go to these other Games, and train other tributes. Since Johanna is a little bit unpredictable, the Capitol hasn't been able to push her to all of the places that they've been able to push the other victors."

She notes that Johanna is very different from Katniss. "Johanna is pretty disgusted by what Katniss is allowing the Capitol to play up. The star-crossed lovers, the wedding, the baby — Johanna would never do that stuff. But she respects Katniss, also, because she's smart. And because she's the leader of the rebellion, like it or not."

Bruno Gunn, who plays Brutus, kept thinking of Cato, the last tribute to die from his district. Bruno was aware that as a past victor, Brutus could even have mentored Cato, giving him advice about

JOHANNA MASON
(JENA MALONE)

how to survive the Games. "I mean, look," says Gunn, "Cato was the last one left in the Games besides Katniss and Peeta, right? *Of course* he had Brutus training him! I'd love to think that Brutus took Cato under his wing."

Meta Golding's character, Enobaria, won her Hunger Games by ripping out another tribute's throat with her teeth. Afterward, she shaved her teeth to sharp points, so that nobody would forget her feat. "Just like Katniss is selling love," says Golding, "Enobaria is selling fierceness."

But even Enobaria has misgivings about going back into the Games. "How does it feel to be in the Quarter Quell?" Golding asks. "Terrible. Humiliating. I mean, I thought I was just going to go back home and be a mentor . . . and that was pretty bad in itself. I want to help the kids in my district, not send them to war! But I've been such a symbol of ferocity, I feel it's my duty to go back into the arena. I'm still strong and I'm still training and I think maybe I can win it again. But it's shocking, and I'm mad."

"Just like Katniss is selling love, Enobaria is selling fierceness."
— Meta Golding

DISTRICT 2 VICTOR ENOBARIA (META GOLDING)

Katniss (Jennifer Lawrence) and Peeta (Josh Hutcherson) stand in front of a Peacekeeper while on the Victory Tour.

GETTING BACK INTO CHARACTER

While the new actors developed their characters for the first time, the returning actors had to consider how their characters had changed and grown since the last movie.

Katniss, for instance, is having nightmares and struggling with the effects of her first round in the arena. Star Jennifer Lawrence puts it like this: "[When the Victory Tour started] Katniss was just getting her life back together. The rule is that, after you win, you don't ever have to be reaped again. It's just unthinkable to her that she'd have to go back into the arena." To access Katniss's feelings, Lawrence read and learned about post-traumatic stress disorder, a debilitating condition that often follows a traumatic experience like fighting in a war.

It's an uncomfortable place for her to be, but Katniss has to learn to trust others and form alliances during the Quarter Quell. Jennifer Lawrence explains: "In the original Games, anyone who is a tribute is an enemy. But in this next round, Haymitch starts to push how important it is to have allies." What Katniss doesn't know, though, is that some alliances are stronger than others, and that some have developed even before the Quarter Quell.

Katniss is more uncomfortable in the environment the Gamemakers have built this time around. "The first Games was in the woods," says Lawrence.

"But this arena is something new to her. A jungle. A sinister jungle."

And — as if it isn't bad enough that Katniss is in shock, in unfamiliar territory, grasping for allies who could stab her in the back — she is also struggling with problems of the heart. Audiences may think she has a simple choice between Peeta and Gale, but Jennifer Lawrence sees it differently. Though Katniss has made deep connections with both of them, at this point neither can give her what she needs. Lawrence says, "There are things about Katniss's life now that Gale doesn't understand — and he used to understand everything. And there are things about her life now that only Peeta can understand. So she has these two parallel lives, and parallel loves." Until she finds a way to sort them out, Katniss feels alone.

Peeta's struggles are different, because he is quicker than Katniss to understand the new political reality. From the beginning of the first film, he's been more aware of what the Capitol demands of the tributes, more aware that they become entirely different people — performers — in the arena. Then, when he comes home alive, he discovers what the Capitol demands of its so-called victors. Josh Hutcherson explains, "Katniss just wants to keep her head down, doesn't want to change things because she wants her family to stay safe. Peeta, on the other hand . . . I don't think he necessarily wants a rebellion, but he wouldn't be completely against it."

"There are things about Katniss's life now that Gale doesn't understand. . . . And there are things about her life now that only Peeta can understand."
— Jennifer Lawrence

The Victory Tour and the Quarter Quell delight the residents of the Capitol, but they enrage Katniss's best friend, Gale. Liam Hemsworth describes his

OPPOSING ATTITUDES

Katniss has complicated relationships with Peeta and Gale, to say the least. Francis Lawrence describes them like this: "Josh and Liam's characters have both expanded in this film. We're getting a better sense of their convictions and philosophies, as well as their intentions with Katniss. Gale represents the need to fight back. The need for rebellion and fighting and even some violence. Peeta represents the opposite. He wants people to figure things out in a nonviolent way, and he's very eloquent. Often, he can solve problems with words.

"Katniss is at home, spending more time with Gale. Still, she has a bond with Peeta because of what they went through together. Katniss is trying to forget everything that happened, but when she's thrown back into the arena it's very easy to look to Peeta, again, for support."

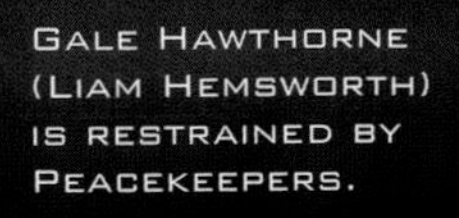

Gale Hawthorne (Liam Hemsworth) is restrained by Peacekeepers.

Primrose Everdeen (Willow Shields) and Buttercup

character like this: "Gale's story line is becoming more complex. He sees the Quarter Quell as yet another betrayal by the Capitol. He's definitely a bigger part of the action now, and you get to see the fire that's been lit inside him. He can't just sit back and watch anymore; he's got to act. Even when Katniss suggests it, he knows that he just can't run away."

Primrose Everdeen, Katniss's sister, must stay behind in District 12 when Katniss goes off to the Victory Tour and, later, the Quarter Quell. But Prim is stronger this time around — more equipped to step up and support their family while Katniss is gone.

Willow Shields, the young actress who plays Prim, reflects on the relationship between the

BUTTERCUP

One character that appears throughout the series is Buttercup — "the world's ugliest cat" as Katniss states in *The Hunger Games* novel. In Suzanne Collins's book, the cat is described as having a "mashed-in nose, half of one ear missing, eyes the color of rotting squash." The cat is absolutely devoted to Prim, but has always distrusted Katniss — ever since she tried to drown him in a bucket when Prim first brought him home as a small, flea-ridden kitten.

In *The Hunger Games: Catching Fire*, however, Buttercup and Katniss do develop a new bond, of sorts, since Buttercup dislikes the Everdeens' new house in the Victor's Village almost as much as Katniss does.

sisters. "As children, their dad died and then their mom kind of goes crazy because of it, so Katniss and Prim become close — and they share this bond and friendship and loyalty because of that. They've always stuck together, and Katniss has always taken care of Prim."

These roles are changing, though, and Prim has been forced to do a lot of growing up. Shields knows that her character has matured a lot since the last film. "Katniss has taught her to help out their family, to help out with their mom. And then of course Prim is becoming a better healer at the same time."

Her role in the community has expanded as well. "Prim is more of a healer in *The Hunger Games: Catching Fire*, like her mom," Shields notes. "She's become a doctor to everyone in District 12."

Effie Trinket — who escorts the District 12 tributes to the Hunger Games each year — may seem like a shallow character at first. Elizabeth Banks, who plays Effie, explains: "Effie really provides a lot of the comic relief in these movies. *The Hunger Games* and *The Hunger Games: Catching Fire* deal with a lot of serious themes and a lot of intense emotional stuff. Effie provides a little levity when it's

EFFIE (ELIZABETH BANKS) AND PEETA (JOSH HUTCHERSON) AT THE PRESIDENT'S PARTY.

Effie Trinket (Elizabeth Banks) on board the train to the Capitol.

WORKING THE CAMERA

Stanley Tucci plays Caesar Flickerman, the television host of the Hunger Games. He is relentlessly upbeat about the Quarter Quell, even as his interviews take an unexpected turn. "You see the juxtaposition between what he does and what's happening in the districts," says Tucci, "and that's pretty disturbing." While unrest is brewing, Flickerman does what he has always done: He interviews tributes before they go into the arena to die. But "Katniss is much more shrewd this time," he says. "She knows how to use Caesar and his broadcast to her best advantage."

time to move away from the tears and the emotion. So I really love being that for this movie."

Still, during *The Hunger Games: Catching Fire*, Effie is slowly evolving as a character. At first, she can't wait to escort Katniss and Peeta on their Victory Tour, showing them off to all of Panem. She has never had a victor from her district — and now she has two! Finally, she's being acknowledged by President Snow and the Capitol, and Effie loves nothing more than being in the spotlight.

Then, suddenly, less than a year later, her tributes are reaped again, sent to almost-certain death. "When the Quarter Quell happens, Effie feels robbed of something very close to her heart," says Elizabeth Banks. "She certainly is a creature of her world, but now she's getting to see it from a different angle and have her eyes opened."

"[The movies] deal with a lot of serious themes and a lot of intense emotional stuff. Effie provides a little levity when it's time to move away from the tears and the emotion."
— Elizabeth Banks

Meanwhile, President Snow regards the Quarter Quell as just another move in a dangerous game. At the end of the first movie, Katniss's act of rebellion challenges the authority of the Capitol, and President Snow knows, better than anyone, how quickly the Capitol could lose control of the districts. "It's a society created by force," says Donald Sutherland, the actor who embodies the president. "There's no generosity. It's like it's made of paper, it's that fragile. One spark can lead to a fire . . . and then it's gone."

While Snow immediately sees that Katniss is dangerous, he also finds her fascinating. Sutherland explains: "He recognizes, almost from the first instant, that no one else has ever been a threat to him, and that Katniss is the manifestation of that threat. A part of him loves it. To be that old and to be suddenly challenged at the end of his life . . . it gives him a kind of delight."

Sutherland's first scene in *The Hunger Games: Catching Fire* is the one in the Everdeen house, where they meet alone for the first time. Snow tells Katniss he was not convinced by the star-crossed lovers' act she performed in the arena, but that her life depends on convincing the rest of Panem that it was real. "It was almost exactly what Suzanne Collins had written," Sutherland remembers. "It was just a joy to do." Sutherland even confesses to having a little affection for Snow, the villain of the story. "I love the precision with which he works."

"It's a society created by force. . . . It's like it's made of paper, it's that fragile. One spark can lead to a fire."
— Donald Sutherland

With the actors in character, a director in place, and a whole army of crew assembled behind the scenes, it was time to start bringing *The Hunger Games: Catching Fire* to life.

President Snow
(Donald Sutherland)

PART 3

EXPANDING THE WORLD OF PANEM

IMAGINING PANEM

The design team of *The Hunger Games: Catching Fire* would need to maintain a look that was continuous with the first film while still breaking new ground in the second. It was an amazing creative opportunity for everybody involved. Director Francis Lawrence says, "I thought it was very important to work with Phil Messina, our production designer, so there was an aesthetic unity to the whole piece. We were never reinventing anything; it was really about expanding so that we were seeing beyond the borders of the last film."

A PRE-PRODUCTION SKETCH OF KATNISS AND PEETA IN DISTRICT 8 ON THE VICTORY TOUR.

Producer Jon Kilik puts it like this: "We needed to start out where we left off with the architecture of the first one, with that strong, graphic, cement style, but build on it and open it up and embrace the requirements of the second book. You have President Snow's mansion, for instance, and a new version of the training quarters . . . these were the kinds of things that had to be related to what we did the first time around."

Phil Messina was looking forward to design challenges like a new Cornucopia and the president's party. "I really loved what we did the first time, but to up it a little . . . that's always fun,"

Woody Harrelson and director Francis Lawrence talk on set.

he says. The larger size and scope of the new film would give him new opportunities for world building. The sequel takes Katniss and Peeta across all of Panem, as well as into more locations inside District 12 and the Capitol. Then it whisks them into an all-new arena, complete with many new obstacles for the tributes.

The Hunger Games: Catching Fire called for more locations in District 12 than *The Hunger Games* had, so Messina and his team would have a chance to explore it further. And what audiences had seen of the Capitol could change quite drastically because, as set decorator Larry Dias points out, "It's a very trendy, temporary society. In the Capitol, they're always coming up with a new spectacle."

One thing they'd need to decide, early on, was whether it would make better sense to shoot on location or to create sets from scratch. Director Lawrence had a firm opinion on this subject, says Nina Jacobson. "Francis absolutely wanted to keep the feeling that these are real things happening to real people. Even though it is the future, it still had to feel immediate and urgent."

Lawrence adds, "When I can, I try to shoot as much as possible in real places, to keep things grounded. The chariot ride, for instance, is almost all created digitally, but we did go and shoot outside on real flat ground, with real horses, keeping it as real as possible within certain parameters."

Place by place, the production design team began to create the scenes described in Collins's novel.

"When I can, I try to shoot as much as possible in real places, to keep things grounded."
— Francis Lawrence

THE LOGISTICS

When you see a movie that is just under two hours long, it can be hard to imagine how many hours of shooting goes into it. *The Hunger Games: Catching Fire* took eighty-nine days to shoot: fifty-six days in the Atlanta area, thirty days in Hawaii, two days in New York, and one day in Los Angeles. There were also — from the people who worked pre-production, to the actors, to the teams of visual effects artists — about 1,500 people involved in the movie from beginning to end.

TOP: CAMERAMEN SET UP TO SHOOT ELIZABETH BANKS (EFFIE TRINKET).
BOTTOM: KEY MAKEUP ARTIST NIKOLETTA SKARLATOS APPLIES CAMOUFLAGE MAKEUP TO THE MALE MORPHLING (JUSTIN HIX).

Katniss (Jennifer Lawrence) barters with a vendor in the Hob.

DISTRICT 12

The production team had its headquarters in Atlanta, Georgia, a large metropolitan area with a lot of variety within its borders, even some patches of countryside. Inside the city limits, they found The Goat Farm Arts Center, a nineteenth-century historic factory that is now an urban organic farm and an artists' community. It was an amazing place to shoot the scenes from District 12.

"They let us take it over," says Francis Lawrence. "We leveled it out, then built our Justice Building there. It worked out really well, because we could have a lot of real stuff right around us, then extend it digitally off to the sides to get a real sense of the mountains and the mining equipment. That way, we could feel the expanse of District Twelve while still staying right in the square."

Also in Atlanta, they found Pullman Yard, an industrial site that was used for servicing trains . . . the perfect place to build the Hob. "The script called not only for the Hob, but also for a shantytown that had sprung up around it," Messina explains. "And this location afforded us all the space for that, with the same character as we had in the first movie. The space was much bigger, though, and we'd need that space to show the Peacekeepers ransacking through. We actually dressed a fairly large space inside — it was like *The Hunger Games* Rose Bowl in there."

Set decorator Larry Dias worked wonders inside the cavernous space, transforming it into something like a flea market, with stalls for the sellers separated by pieces of old pipe. It looked as if some people might even sleep in their stalls, adding to the general feeling of poverty and desperation.

"The shanty village that we set up included not only the Hob but all the people who sort of lived on the fringes. Katniss was in a bad state where she lived before, but the people here are even worse off than she was. So it juxtaposes really well with the Victor's Village," says Messina. "Katniss lives in the village now, but she still feels more comfortable at the Hob."

A shot of the poorest area in District 12

Coal miners head to work from the Seam.

A PRE-PRODUCTION CONCEPT SKETCH OF DISTRICT 12

Joanna Bash
5/23/12

DISTRICT 12: VICTOR'S VILLAGE

In the book, the Victor's Village is described as a series of houses, so Messina imagined twelve identical houses down a single alley. "We wanted them all to be the same, like extravagant workers' housing," he explains. Because District 12 had produced so few victors, most of the houses are empty. Messina explored his ideas in drawings and paintings of this exclusive neighborhood. Even if all the details didn't appear in the movie, he fully imagined what the neighborhood would look like.

Location scouts searched for a new development that might be right to shoot, but ultimately the production team decided to build the ideal village from scratch. For the exteriors, the team built a few facades. Paired with green screens, they would become the external view of the Victor's Village. For the interiors, they built Katniss's entire house on a stage at the Georgia World Congress Center, along with interiors for Peeta's and Haymitch's houses.

The homes are extravagant for District 12, but nothing like the opulent residences of the Capitol. To find inspiration for decorating those sets, Larry Dias imagined he was hired by the Capitol as the victors' interior designer. "So they were sort of model homes, in a way," he says. "Not warm or cozy. They were beautifully decorated, with great furnishings, but they had a sort of spare quality,

A PRE-PRODUCTION SKETCH OF THE DISTRICT 12 VICTOR'S VILLAGE. LEFT: PAULA MALCOMSON (MRS. EVERDEEN) AND WILLOW SHIELDS (PRIMROSE EVERDEEN) DURING A BREAK ON THE SET OF THE EVERDEEN HOUSE IN VICTOR'S VILLAGE.

devoid of any personality or life." He decided that the front of the house, where Katniss doesn't spend much time, would be very formal, and that the character of her family would only be revealed in the kitchen near the back.

"Katniss's furniture was hand-painted with a lot of flora and fauna, symbolic of Katniss and her love of the woods," Dias explains. "I played that up and made it almost as if it was taunting her: Here are these beautiful, woodsy, hand-painted furnishings to remind you of what you can't have. For Peeta's house, we did the masculine version of Katniss's house. And for Haymitch's, well, it's as if he's dismantled the whole thing over the years since he won the Games. It's this boozy, crazy mess."

ABOVE: THE FORMAL LIVING ROOM OF THE EVERDEEN HOUSE. RIGHT: PRIM (WILLOW SHIELDS) AND MRS. EVERDEEN (PAULA MALCOMSON) PREPARE FOOD IN THE KITCHEN OF THEIR NEW HOME — THE MOST LIVED-IN ROOM OF THE HOUSE.

Peeta (Josh Hutcherson) and Katniss (Jennifer Lawrence) meet with Haymitch (Woody Harrelson) in his disorderly house in the Victor's Village.

Crowds hail Peeta (Josh Hutcherson) and Katniss (Jennifer Lawrence) during the Victory Tour.

THE VICTORY TOUR: THE DISTRICTS

When imagining the stops on the Victory Tour, Messina quickly realized that the best use of resources would be to film all the stops in one location. "It was one of those times where we had to show a lot of scale, but we couldn't be going off to different parts of the state to shoot these moments, especially since they appear in a montage," he says. "Eventually we decided that they're probably having this Victory Tour in front of a series of town halls, for the most part. We deviated from that a little, just to give us some variety, but we basically shot all of them in the same place. We shot a real crowd in augmented CG environments. And we used banners to supplement the scenes."

Before the district settings were created digitally, Messina directed what they would look like. His team generated rich, textured concept illustrations of District 4 (Fishing), District 5 (Power), and District 8 (Textiles). They fleshed out District 11 even further, since it was Rue's home, and visiting her district is a painful part of the Victory Tour for Katniss. Messina designed a train station and a city hall for District 11, as well as a glimpse of what it might look like if seen from the window of a train. His images respond to the contrast between the bucolic scene and the police state as described in the book: "Then I see the watchtowers, placed evenly apart, manned with armed guards, so out of place among the fields of wildflowers around them." The beauty of the fields might make a passenger forget, for an instant, that she was hurtling toward a heavily guarded district.

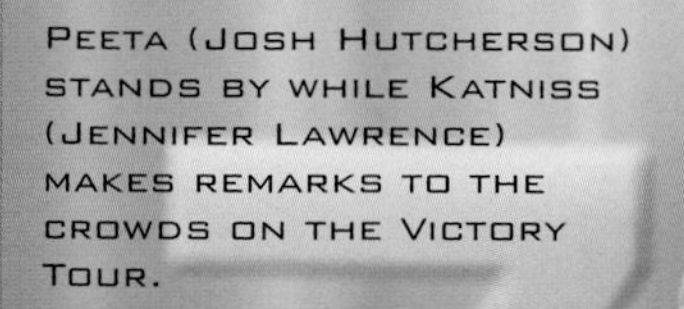

Peeta (Josh Hutcherson) stands by while Katniss (Jennifer Lawrence) makes remarks to the crowds on the Victory Tour.

A line of Peacekeepers

As the production designers worked on expanding the world of Panem, they created this pre-production sketch of the fields of District 11.
Bottom: A pre-production sketch of District 11, featuring displays of Rue and Thresh, tributes who died during the 74th Hunger Games.

THRESH

THE VICTORY TOUR: THE TRAIN

Just as Harry Potter rode the same train to Hogwarts in each of the books and movies, Lawrence and the design team decided that the Capitol's train should remain basically the same. "We just gave it a bit of a face-lift," says Messina.

Larry Dias adds, "We changed the chandelier in the dining car — we got a little more drippy with the crystals, to make it seem more decadent. We also changed the other light fixtures and the table settings, but the dining car was mostly the same."

Katniss's bedroom was altered to reflect the film's darker sensibility, though, with a harsher metallic color scheme.

"And we also built an observation car at the tail end of the train," says Dias. "A car that's completely encased in Deco-inspired glass. It has a silver-and-black metallic theme, really quite beautiful." From this car, Katniss and Peeta can see all of Panem . . . and all of Panem can see them.

A shot of the luxurious train car that brings the victors to the Capitol.
Opposite: Katniss (Jennifer Lawrence) and Effie (Elizabeth Banks) in the train on their way to the Capitol.

Effie (Elizabeth Banks) escorts Peeta (Josh Hutcherson) and Katniss (Jennifer Lawrence) to the party at President Snow's mansion.

A fire-breather at the party

PRESIDENT SNOW'S MANSION: THE PARTY

One of the most challenging — and exciting — set pieces of the movie would be the lavish party held in the banquet room of President Snow's mansion, at the end of the Victory Tour. It is an extravagant affair, where Katniss and Peeta are face-to-face with the beautiful but baffling people of the Capitol.

The party was filmed at the Swan House, an elegant classical mansion built in the heart of Atlanta in 1928 by Edward and Emily Inman, the heirs to a cotton fortune. It sits in a busy neighborhood, set back from the street by a long driveway, a cascading fountain, a terraced lawn, and gorgeous formal gardens. As Elizabeth Banks puts it, "We're imagining a future world, but we are basing it on places from the past. You can really imagine that it would survive through hundreds of years of turmoil."

"The outrageousness of the party comes from the people of the Capitol and not necessarily from the architecture."
— Phil Messina

THE PRESIDENTIAL FEAST

The astonishing feast was inspired by a table Phil Messina had seen once at a runway show, but many times bigger. The idea was to show a sheer abundance of food, more than Katniss and Peeta could imagine or make sense of. As Katniss says in the novel, "The real star of the evening is the food. . . . Everything you can think of, and things you have never dreamed of, lie in wait." While back in their districts, people are starving, in the Capitol, people are making themselves throw up so they can gorge on ever more food. The bounty is appealing and appalling at the same time.

Larry Dias created the actual buffet tables — all two hundred feet of them. He remembers: "I worked with Rick Riggs, our painter. We came up with a resin that we tinted, and did a process on a reflective laminate, so it was like a mirrored backing with a tinted solution over the top, that dried to a hard finish. And that became the style for the tabletops." The accessories that were used for the food were important, too. Dias explains, "I created some tiered platters that were outfitted with LED interiors, so they glowed, and I found thirty or forty candelabra that we scattered around the table. And we used a lot of stemware, glassware, and crystal to create this truly decadent environment." The team even created labels for the special-edition champagne that would be served at this extravaganza.

Food stylist Jack White was in charge of creating the feast itself. It would need to look like an abundant amount of food — enough for a huge number of people, including over two hundred party guests, forty musicians, twelve Avoxes, and fire-breathers and presidential guards. It needed to look unusual, like food Katniss might never have seen before, but also like something she (or the audience) might potentially want to eat.

White shakes his head in amazement and says, "We've got suckling pigs. And there's a couple of ribs on this platter that are actually part of the cow. You know in *The Flintstones*, when they bring that big thing up and set it on the car? That's what we've got here."

White searched for real foods that had an exotic edge. "We have star fruit, and pepino melons, and cherimoyas, and baby pineapples, and a lot of champagne grapes. I'm crazy excited about the way it all looks."

Colored projections on the walls of the Swan House created a futuristic backdrop for President Snow's party.

Phil Messina says, "Initially, the Swan House was pitched by the location department as a house for the Victor's Village, but it was too big to be used for that. After a while, I came up with the idea that maybe . . . we could use the exterior for the president's party, because the grounds were so amazing." The design team ended up constructing a no-holds-barred set on the grounds of the Swan House, as well as taking over several of its rooms for interior shots.

"Snow is a little bit of an old-school guy, so the fact that he has this elegant house in the middle of a park, with the grand city in the distance . . . that felt just right to us," Messina continues. "The outrageousness of the party comes from the people of the Capitol and not necessarily from the architecture. Snow's house is almost like the White House, with its classical detailing symbolizing power."

While the house itself is traditional, Messina hit upon an unexpected idea to bring the Swan House into the future. "I came across this piece of reference on building projections, where you actually project animated 3-D images onto structures. I showed it to Francis, who really dug it, and we ended up hiring a company to do the projections for us. So we have the grounding of the classical architecture, but the images turn it pink and purple and blue."

The Hunger Games: Catching Fire's team built a stone staircase leading up to the center of the mansion, as well as a grand set of gates.

Preparations for the president's party were as over-the-top as anything you might find in the Capitol. Larry Dias says, "There was a traditional fountain surrounded by formal gardens, so we built tables that fit among the boxwood trees." The team also built a dance floor, illuminated with light structures designed by Messina.

PRESIDENT SNOW'S MANSION: SNOW'S QUARTERS

The interior of the Swan House was also the location for the shots of President Snow's private quarters. Messina's team removed the furnishings from three rooms and replaced them with decor of the kind that Snow might have. Larry Dias describes the style as "very classic, sort of dictatorial. He's surrounded by antiques and crystal chandeliers and other finery."

Coincidentally, the Swan House already had a bird theme — which the team could build on for *The Hunger Games: Catching Fire.* If you look very closely at the pictures in Snow's office, you might spot what looks like a Victorian sketch from nature, complete with a Latin genus and species name beneath. But it's not a drawing of a creature that lived in Victorian times or any times: It's a jabberjay.

PRESIDENT SNOW EATS WITH HIS GRANDDAUGHTER, A BOUQUET OF WHITE ROSES — HIS FAVORITE FLOWER — GRACING THE TABLE.

And, because white roses are Snow's personal favorite, there are bouquets of them all over his quarters. "The white rose is the symbol of purity," says Dias. "The exact opposite of who Snow is."

PLUTARCH HEAVENSBEE (PHILIP SEYMOUR HOFFMAN) MEETS WITH PRESIDENT SNOW (DONALD SUTHERLAND) IN HIS OFFICE. AN IMAGE OF A JABBERJAY SITS ON THE TABLE AT THE FAR RIGHT OF THE PHOTO.

THE SWAN HOUSE

Built in 1928, the Swan House is one of Atlanta's architectural gems. It was commissioned by Edward and Emily Inman, a prominent and wealthy local couple, and designed by American classical architect Philip Trammell Shutze. Today it is an important part of the Atlanta History Center.

Mrs. Inman owned two swan tables that historians believe were the inspiration for the swan motif that runs throughout the house, from the entryway to the dressing room.

Jessica Rast Van Landuyt, the manager of the Swan House, says, "Mrs. Inman certainly did not want a modern home. The Inmans had traveled extensively throughout Europe, and saw all the English estates and Italian villas, and knew that's what they wanted for their dream home."

The house was designed to be approached in an automobile — new at the time — up a long and elegant driveway. The front of the house has a grand, Italianate style, impressive to visitors. But when the driver continues along the driveway, he or she comes to a more intimate entrance in the Palladian style, drawn from the architecture of ancient Greece and Rome.

The Inmans' youngest son had just left for college when they began to design the house, so family life was not paramount in their plans. The upstairs of the home has only four bedrooms, evidence that they were not expecting many guests to stay overnight. The downstairs of the house, however, is a series of grand rooms designed for entertaining on a lavish and generous scale.

A party could extend onto the grounds of the mansion, as it does in *The Hunger Games: Catching Fire*. The Swan House has thirty-three acres of land, which encompasses gardens, terraced lawns, boxwood trees, and cascading fountains.

The Swan House was excited to have the filmmakers use their property, and make an already beautiful garden sparkle even more.

The atrium of the Atlanta Marriott Marquis, designed by architect John C. Portman

THE TRAINING CENTER: KATNISS'S QUARTERS

Before shooting the first *The Hunger Games* movie, Phil Messina had come across photos of the huge hotel atrium at Atlanta's Marriott Marquis. Its intimidating design immediately struck him as perfect for the Capitol, but the shoot was taking place in North Carolina, so practical considerations kept him from using it in the first film. When Atlanta became the base of operations for *The Hunger Games: Catching Fire*, he knew just where he would set the Training Center, the building where the tributes live and train while they're in the Capitol.

> **"The scale of [the Marriott] is perfect. It feels like you're in the belly of the beast." — Phil Messina**

"The Capitol is all about something new, so we started thinking about how they would have organized these Games," he says. "[Quarter Quells] are like all-star games, so definitely there's a new training center, new apartment. New everything."

When the Marriott was designed in 1985 by architect John C. Portman, the atrium was the largest in the world, with two vertical chambers soaring up for fifty-two stories, creating an overwhelming sense of space. After the parade, Katniss and the other tributes take an elevator back to their quarters, and in that scene the atrium of the Marriott is visible. "The scale of it is perfect," says Messina. "It feels like you're in the belly of the beast, which is great for us thematically." Its heavy style also fit stylistically with elements from the previous film.

Messina continues: "And then the location manager showed me an empty floor. It's actually the tenth floor — it's like a function floor. It just doesn't have rooms on it. It's open to the windows and the idea dawned on us to build Katniss's apartment there and have real environment out the windows. So we built it on the tenth floor of a functioning hotel."

In this pre-production sketch, a hovercraft lands on the roof of the Training Center in the Capitol.

Francis Lawrence loved this whole idea. "You get some of the depth and scope of the real Marriott," he explains, "so you don't feel boxed in by a set that might be on a stage, or having a green screen in the background. You have life with Peacekeepers and elevators going up and down in the background, and even though it's in soft focus and in the background you just feel like you're in a real place."

Larry Dias fleshed out the set so that it felt like a place where Katniss could live. "In the last movie, the apartment was colorful and a little bit bolder in its design," he says. "This time, we muted it down and played with metallics, lots of softer tones. I found a modular sofa that cascades down and has a very topographic quality about it, which was interesting because it mimicked the design of the Cornucopia. Then, over that sofa, we hung a picture that had four-by-four cubes on a wire grid, reminiscent of the dome that is exposed at the end of the movie."

Messina's team even imagined a hovercraft landing pad on the roof of the Training Center. They developed the idea in drawings and paintings and created it with visual effects. In the background of that scene, audiences will see the view from the rooftop of the Marriott in Atlanta, surrounded by other striking buildings designed by the same architect.

Katniss (Jennifer Lawrence) inside the hovercraft that will take her to the arena.

Peeta (Josh Hutcherson) and Katniss (Jennifer Lawrence) in their quarters at the Training Center.

Peeta (Josh Hutcherson) and Katniss (Jennifer Lawrence) in the Training Center.

THE TRAINING CENTER: THE GYM

The tributes' Training Center gymnasium was not filmed at the Marriott, but at the Georgia World Congress Center nearby. Like the Training Center in the first film, it was a place where tributes would hone the skills they'd need in the arena, from mastering weaponry to learning the basics of survival in the wild. This time the place had a different feeling, however. Dias says, "The Training Center is less of an innocent place this time. In the first Games, they're a bunch of kids coming in. This time, it's the old diehards coming back, so it's less of a training facility."

Enobaria (Meta Golding) wields a sword during practice in the Training Center.

The film crew is in place to capture Jennifer Lawrence (Katniss) taking a shot.

Francis Lawrence and Jennifer Lawrence (Katniss) on set in District 12.

"The scope of this production was very large and complex. One day we'd be out with five characters in forty-degree water, making a volcanic rock island spin; the next day we'd be in a town square with five hundred extras; the next day burning down a building; the next moving train cars through a forest. The cool thing about it is that the complex pieces were all there to service a really emotional, powerful story."
—Francis Lawrence

ON LOCATION

Shooting in Atlanta presented occasional problems, like the ordinary urban noise. "It seemed like we always had trains or subways racing nearby," Francis Lawrence remembers, "so we were constantly ducking and dodging the sound. It could get a little difficult when people were giving speeches on Victory Tours and things like that." Overall, though, Atlanta was the perfect location for shooting the district and Capitol scenes. The team spent fifty-six days, in all, on location in Georgia.

Once they were wrapped, it was time to move to a new set of sequences — those in the arena.

Woody Harrelson (Haymitch) prepares to shoot a scene with Patrick St. Esprit, the actor who plays the new head Peacekeeper of District 12, Romulus Thread.

PART 4

DESIGNING THE ARENA

This pre-production sketch shows the arena from above, with the Cornucopia on the island at the very center.

The ground is too bright and shiny and keeps undulating. I squint down at my feet and see that my metal plate is surrounded by blue waves that lap up over my boots. Slowly I raise my eyes and take in the water spreading out in every direction. . . . This is no place for a girl on fire.

— Catching Fire

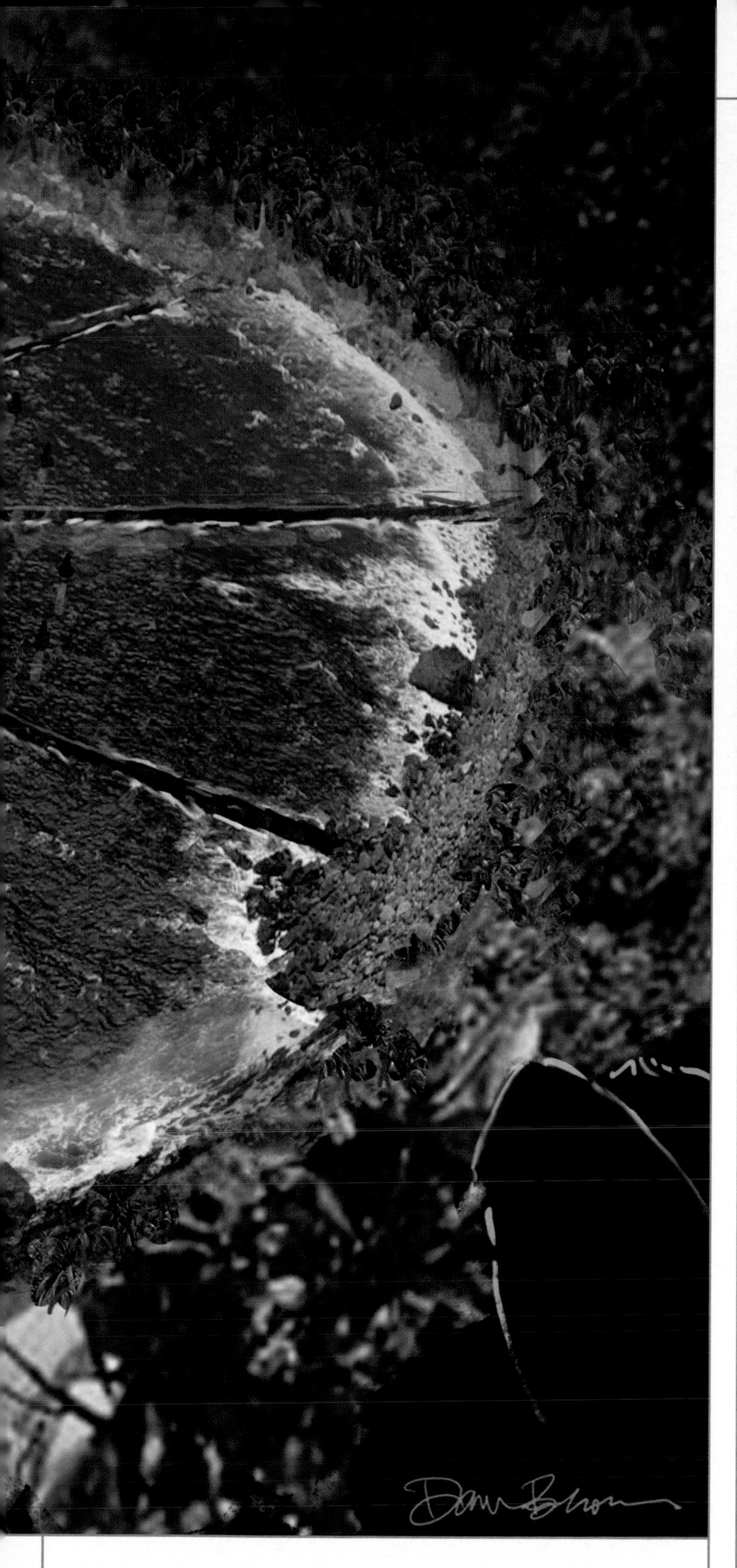

KATNISS (JENNIFER LAWRENCE) IN THE ARENA.

THE ARENA

When Katniss Everdeen emerges into the arena, she's briefly disoriented, then surveys the territory around her to get a sense of what she's up against: There's the Cornucopia, sitting on a small island. Surrounding that is salt water, turquoise and sparkling in the sun. Thin strips of land radiate out from the island, like spokes on a wheel. Between each set of spokes are two tributes, standing on small metal plates. And surrounding it all, beyond the water — a strip of beach, and then lush, dense jungle.

"The arena itself plays a larger role in this story than even some of the other tributes do," says Francis Lawrence. "It's a much more interactive, stylized place. The tributes are raised up on these elevators out into the middle of water, so to even begin the Games they have to dive in and swim and climb across some volcanic rocks. This arena is much trickier than the last one, and the Gamemakers have built many secrets into it."

When approaching the arena scenes, *The Hunger Games: Catching Fire*'s team determined that they would need to shoot in two places. The initial fighting at the Cornucopia could be done in Atlanta, but for the rest they decided on Hawaii, a location that could truly capture the tropical feel of the arena.

ATLANTA: THE CORNUCOPIA

However, even before a shooting location could be chosen, the Cornucopia had to be designed. And production designer Phil Messina faced a major decision: whether or not to use the same one as in the previous film. "I had many discussions with Francis about whether the Cornucopia should look the same as in the first movie, or whether it should be something that changes with the arena," Messina says. "Finally we asked ourselves, 'How would the Gamemakers approach this?' Since the Capitol is a sort of disposable society, where something new is always better, we decided to try something different."

But making that choice was only the first step. If the structure didn't look like the previous Cornucopia, what would it look like? Messina's gut feeling was that it could move a little further from the kind of cornucopia that might appear on a Thanksgiving table. This time, he could get more abstract.

"I did endless sketches and illustrations," he recalls. "You should see what I threw away! But one of the main inspirations was a book that Bryan Unkeless had given me, about these Soviet monuments. They're made of concrete and most of them are sort of left out in the landscape, getting decrepit. There was one that had fallen apart — it was almost in shards — it just spoke to me; it felt right for what we were trying to do. And then for the finish, I looked at the work of another artist, Anish Kapoor, who does a lot of metallic sculptures, way-cool stuff, where space sort of turns inside out. So his work gave me the idea that we could chrome this Cornucopia, almost make it look like it fell out of space and landed on this rock. All together, the hope is that you can sort of feel the motion in the structure . . . even before it starts spinning."

"The hope is that you can sort of feel the motion in the structure . . . even before it starts spinning."
— Phil Messina

In the book, the Cornucopia sits on a sandy island, but Francis Lawrence and Phil Messina came up with the idea that it should sit on a rock island that would feel harsh and foreboding, not something peaceful with water lapping against the sand. "We decided to make the island an immediate symbol of what the tributes would face," Messina explains. "Something threatening and challenging."

The Cornucopia, sitting on a rocky island, as imagined in a pre-production sketch.

Two abandoned Soviet monuments that served as inspiration for the Cornucopia

Early on, they discussed putting it in a water tank to film it. It would be simple enough to extend the water with visual effects in post-production. However, it was important to Francis Lawrence to film whatever possible "practically" — that is, in an actual setting. And as luck would have it, the perfect location presented itself.

"Our location manager found this water park that was built for the 1996 Olympics," Messina says, referring to Clayton County International Park. "It's a big circular body of water that's man-made. It happened to close at the end of the season — Labor Day — so we took it over, drained it, built our island in the middle of it, built our scenery, and filled it

THE TEAM CREATED THE CORNUCOPIA IN A MAN-MADE LAKE AT THE CLAYTON COUNTY INTERNATIONAL PARK. HERE YOU CAN SEE THE CORNUCOPIA ON THE CENTRAL ISLAND, WITH SOME OF THE SPOKES AND PEDESTALS.

"Tick, tock, the arena's a clock."
— *Catching Fire*

back up." They also built some of the spokes that separate the different sections of the arena, and some of the pedestals for the victors to launch from at the beginning of the Quarter Quell.

One of the features of the Cornucopia is that the Gamemakers make the island it sits on spin, disorienting any tributes who happen to be on it. In order to create this effect in the film, the team placed

"When I was writing the book, I really wasn't thinking about how spinning the tributes on the island might one day translate into watching a group of wet, shivering actors being spun repeatedly on a large disc while performing their hearts out." — Suzanne Collins

the Cornucopia on a disc, like a merry-go-round. Special effects coordinator Steve Cremin explains, "It would spin at a speed that generated enough centrifugal force that people would have a hard time holding on to it, while still being safe enough for our cast." Filming this effect with the actors, rather than creating it through special effects, created extra intensity in this scene.

As it happened, Suzanne Collins was on set the day they shot this part of the film. She says, "When I was writing the book, I really wasn't thinking about how spinning the tributes on the island might one day translate into watching a group of wet, shivering actors being spun repeatedly on a large disc while performing their hearts out. I felt slightly guilty. And dizzy. And very grateful for how game and talented they were. The end result is fantastic."

After wrapping in Atlanta, the cast and crew prepared to shift locations. It was a welcome break, since winter had arrived in Georgia. *The Hunger Games: Catching Fire*'s team gladly took off for Hawaii to shoot the rest of the Quarter Quell arena scenes.

PEETA (JOSH HUTCHERSON) CLINGS TO THE ROCKY ISLAND AS IT BEGINS TO SPIN.

Jennifer Lawrence as Katniss crawls up the island toward the Cornucopia as the cameras roll.

In the opening moments of the 75th Hunger Games, Katniss (Jennifer Lawrence) aims her arrow at Finnick Odair (Sam Claflin).

HAWAII: THE JUNGLE

While the Atlanta area offered a wide variety of urban and rural settings, Francis Lawrence knew that he'd need something different for the arena. The perfect location turned out to be Hawaii, where he could find the look of complete wilderness but in a very safe environment.

Producer Nina Jacobson says, "To capture the

action of the arena, we needed a true tropical forest. We wanted the big leaves — we wanted it to look exotic. No place came close to Hawaii in terms of giving that juxtaposition of jungle right up next to beach. So we took advantage of that incredible geography."

"There's a lot of varied terrain here, so we can have different kinds of environments within the jungle itself to shoot in," Francis Lawrence explains. From the gorgeous beaches to the lush and rainy jungle canopy, Hawaii provided them with an ideal arena. To further take advantage of this incredible setting, the team decided to use a special kind of camera to convey the arena on the big screen.

FINNICK (SAM CLAFLIN), PEETA (JOSH HUTCHERSON), AND KATNISS (JENNIFER LAWRENCE) TAKE STOCK OF OBSTACLES IN THE ARENA.

DIRECTOR FRANCIS LAWRENCE AND PRODUCER NINA JACOBSON ON SET IN ATLANTA.

"To capture the action of the arena, we needed a true tropical forest. We wanted the big leaves — we wanted it to look exotic. No place came close to Hawaii in terms of giving that juxtaposition of jungle right up next to beach."
— Nina Jacobson

Katniss (Jennifer Lawrence) and Peeta (Josh Hutcherson) share an intimate moment in the arena.

THE CHALLENGES OF THE ARENA

All in all, the cast and crew spent about six weeks in Hawaii, re-creating the terrifying challenges the victors face in the arena during the Quarter Quell. "We spent the first week shooting on a beach, which was really nice," says director Lawrence. "We had a couple of moments where the tide came up higher than we thought and washed away some of our set, but we regrouped."

Shooting in the jungle was more complicated. Lawrence continues, "The days are short because you're under the canopy and in the canyons. Plus we were shooting those scenes with our IMAX

THE FILM CREW SETS UP FOR A SCENE AT DUSK ON OAHU.

cameras, which are large, bulky cameras. It could get sort of tricky going over slippery rocks and trudging through the jungle."

The arena scenes would inevitably require more visual effects to be added in post-production when the shoot was over. Still, Lawrence and his team did everything possible to guarantee the authenticity and develop the emotional impact of the arena's set pieces.

"For me the action sequences get defined by an emotional value, even if that's not the first thing that comes to mind when you think of an action sequence," Lawrence says. "Each one should feel different, experientially. There are story elements taking place in each one, moving the plot forward. And there are character moments, ideally, so you can see some character growth in each sequence, some change in the relationships."

One of the first obstacles the tributes face is a raging lightning storm. Erik Feig recalls, "The lightning storm is built around a beautiful, actual bona fide banyan tree, this gorgeous tree that's been there forever — actually, that tree was one of the major reasons we picked that location. The lightning is a CG effect, but everything else in that scene, including the explosion, was shot practically."

At that point, the characters are still in a state of shock, not yet accustomed to the arena. As other obstacles come at them, though, the victors begin to try to make sense of what's around them. Their characters grow as they start to understand what they're up against. Alliances among the characters develop and shift.

"The lightning storm is built around a beautiful, actual bona fide banyan tree, this gorgeous tree that's been there forever."
— Erik Feig

Soon after the lightning storm, red rain pours down on the tributes. This sequence was shot on the beach in Hawaii, with Johanna, Beetee, and Wiress running onto the sand in a panic, covered in blood created by the team's makeup artists. Audiences won't see the rain coming down, but rather its effect: confusion.

Later, the victors are pursued by a billowing fog that turns out to be poisonous, leaving gruesome and painful welts on the skin of whomever it slips around. On set, makeup artist Ve Neill created

Erik Feig, President of Production of the Lionsgate Motion Picture Group and Josh Hutcherson on set in Hawaii.

Katniss (Jennifer Lawrence) stands at the ready, a genuine banyan tree behind her.

lifelike, oozing blisters. The actors performed in a fog created by the crew, and additional fog was added digitally in post-production. For director Francis Lawrence, the emotional message of this sequence was about sacrifice and loss, in addition to the adrenaline rush of trying to outrun the fog.

Lawrence recalls, "Then there's a sequence with these really vicious and aggressive monkeys in the jungle, and so we based the monkeys on real monkeys called drills. They're very dangerous and aggressive, though — pretty much untrainable. There's no way to use real monkeys to fight with our characters.

"So we find a real place in the jungle, and we have our actors fight with things that aren't there.

Johanna (Jena Malone) after the blood rain.
Above: Key hairstylist Joe Matke and hair department head Linda Flowers with the Female Morphling (Megan Hayes).

Katniss (Jennifer Lawrence) and Peeta (Josh Hutcherson) submerge Finnick (Sam Claflin) in the water to detoxify him after he was exposed to a poisonous fog.

Katniss (Jennifer Lawrence) and Finnick (Sam Claflin) in the arena before the monkey attack.

We try to make it as real as possible by having stand-in people fight a bit, and run through the sequences with the actors; the animals get added in later in post-production. Since we based our creatures on real animals, though, we have a whole behavioral vocabulary to pull from. It's not entirely fantasy, and I think it all comes together to create a very realistic sequence." Above all, the encounter with the monkeys sows fear among the tributes.

When they see a tsunami in the distance, Katniss and her allies are in awe. Of this moment, the director says, "The tsunami is happening in a place that the characters aren't in, so it's something they witness from afar. It's pretty spectacular in terms of its sound and size, coming down through the jungle and out into the lagoon, and up against the Cornucopia. It's one of the moments that helps our characters figure out what's going on in the arena."

"The jabberjays are a different sort of Capitol invention. The threat is psychological. The Capitol really messes with your mind and tortures you."
— Francis Lawrence

And one of the final terrors of the arena is the discovery of a group of jabberjays in the jungle, mimicking the voices of people the tributes have left back home. "The jabberjay sequence is different from the other ones, in that it's not so visceral," says Lawrence. "The other ones are so filled with action — for example, the fog can burn your skin, and it's billowing down this hillside, and you've got to run for your life. Or the monkeys are attacking, and they could really kill you. But the jabberjays are a different sort of Capitol invention. The threat is psychological. The Capitol really messes with your mind and tortures you. We needed to make that scene emotionally unbearable for the characters."

After about six weeks, cast and crew left the tropics to return home, while Lawrence and his team turned to the task of post-production work, making every frame of their film shine.

Director Francis Lawrence confers with Steadicam operator David Thompson, who is using a Steadicam-mounted IMAX camera.

LIFE ON SET

When the cast first gathered for shooting in Atlanta, it was like a reunion for many of the actors. "When I got there, everyone was freaking out because I was so much taller," says Willow Shields, the actress who plays Primrose Everdeen. "They didn't even recognize me!"

Almost right away, a real camaraderie and connection built between the cast members. Many of them were staying at the same hotel in Atlanta, which made it easy to mingle or grab a meal together. Some of the stars had the chance to relax with a visit to the Georgia Aquarium. And once again, Josh Hutcherson made sure there was a basketball hoop for the actors to use when they were off-camera.

Just like in the movie, the tributes tended to stick together. They knew one another from training, and most of their scenes were together — so their downtime was usually at the same time, too. They took advantage of the Atlanta location to go to the Cirque du Soleil premiere of *TOTEM*.

It was different from the shoot of *The Hunger Games*, though, because while the first movie had a large teen cast, now the tributes were people of all ages. One benefit of the diverse cast was that there were greater opportunities for older actors to mentor younger ones, and the younger ones to soak up their experience.

Sam Claflin (Finnick) and Lynn Cohen (Mags) shared a particularly tight bond that grew from their characters' relationship. Mags volunteers for the Quarter Quell when Finnick's one true love, Annie, is chosen. Mags knows Finnick well enough to understand that Annie means everything to him. He might not care about his own life, but he wants for Annie to survive at all costs. Mags goes into the Games with little hope of returning, but Finnick does all he can to repay her noble gesture by looking out for her in the arena. "I almost feel like I have that relationship with Lynn now. I'd do anything for her. Even carry her over a mountain . . ." Claflin says.

Many of the actors were in awe of Philip Seymour Hoffman when he arrived on set. Josh Hutcherson says, "Just watching him was like going to an acting class."

Shooting in Atlanta in November, after Hurricane Sandy blew through the East Coast, created some unexpected circumstances. Atlanta was spared, but the temperatures plummeted. To keep warm, the actors kept heavy coats on until the last possible second, and space heaters were scattered around the set. Inflatable Jacuzzis full of warm water awaited cast members when they emerged from shooting the Cornucopia scene.

The experience in Hawaii was completely different. In Atlanta night shoots for the Capitol party had gone into the early hours of the morning, but in Hawaii filming wrapped when the sun set at seven o'clock. There, the cast was in a more remote jungle location. They stayed in trailers, shooting whenever they could, and taking lots of breaks to let bouts of rain sweep past.

No matter the location, cast and crew felt supported by director Lawrence. Producer Jon Kilik says, "He's got a great imagination, he's got great shot selection, he's got great vision, and he's great with the actors."

Author Suzanne Collins observed him at work, and loved what she saw. "Francis is an amazing director," she says. "It's not just how beautifully he opens up the world of Panem or brings the rising rebellion to life or takes you into a stunning and sinister arena. For me the greatest achievement is how powerfully he brings Katniss's emotional and dramatic arc to the screen. With all the visual richness and dynamic action, her journey is the beating heart of the film."

Under Lawrence's direction, long days of shooting flew by.

USING IMAX

Director Francis Lawrence chose to show the arena portion of the movie — from the moment Katniss goes up in the elevator until the moment the Games come to a close — in IMAX, and so much of that section was shot using IMAX film. His intention was to capture the experience of the arena, with its heightened senses and constant fear. Katniss rushes up in the elevator and the doors open to reveal a world of greater clarity and detail — it's as if Dorothy has entered a twisted Oz.

As producer Nina Jacobson says, "The imagination of Suzanne Collins needs a big canvas, and

A MIX OF HANDHELD AND TRIPOD IMAX CAMERAS ARE USED TO CREATE THIS SHOT OF KATNISS (JENNIFER LAWRENCE) IN THE ARENA.

we're taking advantage of the biggest canvas there is in a movie theater. It's a particularly good match of medium and message."

IMAX stands for Image Maximus, or maximum image. Most films are shot with 35-millimeter film, in which an image is compressed into a small, square frame and then expanded by a film projector to fit a movie screen. The size of the frame is much larger with IMAX film — 70 millimeters high — which allows for double the quality of the resolution. The film size gives an IMAX movie exponentially more clarity than a movie shot in 35-millimeter film. "You see every detail," says producer Jon Kilik. "And if you see it in an IMAX theater, you see it on a screen that's a hundred feet high."

The format would allow extra-wide shots as well as extreme close-ups. And unlike standard film, with its square frame, IMAX film has more vertical space. It would be the perfect format, then, for showcasing the great height of the trees around Katniss in the tropical forest.

In *The Hunger Games: Catching Fire*, the film's format would expand just as the characters entered the arena, offering greater detail and greater immersion in their experience. And also, as producer Jacobson notes, IMAX would be perfect for shooting the action scenes of the arena rather than the more character-driven scenes in the first half of the movie.

The IMAX film requires an incredible, detail-rich set. As IMAX technician Doug Lavender explains, "Normally you would have to do an awful lot of set decoration to make everything as full of detail and rich color and interesting textures as you would need for the IMAX format. The rain forest in Hawaii, only moments from a big city, is pre-done by nature. It's fantastic because it naturally has so much detail and life in it."

VFX DATA WRANGLERS COLLECT LIGHTING REFERENCE FOR AN IMAX CABLE SHOT.

The crew used cable cams to get the IMAX cameras flying through the forest to capture the dramatic combat scenes, as well as a mix of cranes and handheld cameras. "Very few directors have used handheld IMAX cameras," Doug Lavender notes.

Francis Lawrence says that as a director, he's always thinking about the experience the audience is having in the theater. "The more immersive it can be, the better," he says. "So to be able to use IMAX to open the world up in a much bigger way, when the characters are diving somewhere new, is really exciting to me."

"To be able to use IMAX to open the world up in a much bigger way . . . is really exciting to me."
— Francis Lawrence

PART 5

CREATING COSTUMES, DESIGNING FACES

THE LOOK OF *THE HUNGER GAMES: CATCHING FIRE*

Francis Lawrence knew costume designer Trish Summerville from their work together on music videos, and Summerville had recently received wide acclaim for her costumes in *The Girl with the Dragon Tattoo*. As soon as she joined the *The Hunger Games: Catching Fire* team, she and Lawrence sat down to discuss developing the characters' wardrobes.

"Francis and I talked about making the look a tad darker, a bit more chic, a bit more fashion-forward," Summerville remembers. "Not comical, but keeping that weird, perverse sense that the Capitol has." For the scenes that showed life in the Capitol, Summerville felt it was important to show a variety of images. "Fashion changes quickly in the Capitol, and I realized we could have a lot of diversity in the people there. I didn't want everybody to look like they shopped at the same store, but show different trends and subcultures." And even characters who did not live in the Capitol would be influenced by those tastes, as the victors' clothing would come from the Capitol.

Ultimately, Summerville used a combination of other designers' work and her own designs to create signature looks for all the characters in the film. Returning makeup artist Ve Neill and hair designer Linda Flowers would complement the costumes with their own artistry. As Neill says, "This movie is a makeup artist's dream! I mean, you have everything

here from high-fashion couture beauty makeup to special effects makeup. We have blood, we have fantasy, we have Effie, who's like a whole world unto herself. We have characters from all the districts . . . I could go on and on."

Inspiration came from runway shows, magazines, websites, other movies, and the *Catching Fire* book itself. Slowly but surely, new looks began to emerge.

CAPITOL RESIDENTS, DRESSED IN PANEM'S LATEST FASHIONS, GATHER FOR THE PRESIDENT'S PARTY.
OPPOSITE: CAESAR FLICKERMAN (STANLEY TUCCI) INTERVIEWS BEETEE (JEFFREY WRIGHT).

"Francis and I talked about making the look a tad darker, a bit more chic, a bit more fashion-forward."
— Trish Summerville

Katniss (Jennifer Lawrence) wears simple clothes when home in District 12.

KATNISS EVERDEEN

In *The Hunger Games: Catching Fire*, Katniss is savvy enough to understand that there's meaning in the way she looks, that she can communicate through her clothing. Summerville's challenge was to show at once that the Games have changed Katniss, that she's not the innocent she once was, yet that she is still the same person at her core.

As Summerville sees it, Katniss is careful to keep her look appropriate to her surroundings. When she's home, for example, she is dressed more or less the same as always. "We wanted to carry over the iconic piece, the hunting jacket," Summerville says. "We aged it a bit more because it's six months later. But we wanted to keep the original Katniss alive even though she's a victor now, with money and a house in the Victor's Village. She would never dress up too much around the people of her district."

When she embarks on the Victory Tour, however, her clothes are suddenly a bit more fashionable. Katniss allows the Capitol to have its way with her clothes, while never crossing the line into completely outlandish. As Summerville puts it, "We see Katniss go from District Twelve, where she fits, to the Capitol, where she doesn't. She takes a journey, and we can see the journey in her clothing, too."

While Katniss is in the Capitol, certain themes tie her clothing and hairstyles together. Summerville incorporated fire and feathers into many of her outfits, for instance, since she's the Girl on Fire as well as the Mockingjay. "In the dress for the party, we incorporated flames and feathers, in reds and blacks," Summerville explains. "And for the Mockingjay

THE VICTORY TOUR WARDROBE FOR THE DISTRICT 12 VICTORS, PEETA (JOSH HUTCHERSON) AND KATNISS (JENNIFER LAWRENCE), IS FASHIONABLE BUT NOT OUTLANDISH.

dress, I found images of a certain type of peacock with these iridescent blue feathers. With one of our sketch artists, I compiled all these photos together to make a pattern, and then incorporated that pattern into the clothes."

The looks that Summerville devised for Katniss actually helped Jennifer Lawrence get into character each day. "The costume is very important to an actor," she explains. "I totally understand that feeling of wearing things where you don't understand how you look and you're not used to feeling your body a certain way. Some of the Capitol clothes are so out of place, they put Katniss in that uncomfortable position, feeling out of control of her own body."

Katniss's braid remains her signature look, says hair designer Linda Flowers, but she wears it differently

"The costume is very important to an actor. . . . Some of the Capitol clothes are so out of place, they put Katniss in that uncomfortable position, feeling out of control of her own body."
— Jennifer Lawrence

GALE HAWTHORNE

Costume designer Trish Summerville says, "In the districts, it's about function and not fashion. I wanted to keep the colors of Gale's clothing really subdued. When he's with Katniss, he's a little bit more pulled together, trying to make a good impression. I wanted him to appear a bit softer in those scenes. For the coal mining scenes, though, I tried to keep it realistic."

KATNISS EVERDEEN, PLAYED BY JENNIFER LAWRENCE

in *The Hunger Games: Catching Fire*. "The braid is for hunting, but you see her get away from it a little here. Instead, you'll see different types of braids, like four-strand braids and fishbone braids. There's a little bit of braids everywhere. It's one way that Katniss defies the Capitol, sticking to her braids."

Likewise, her makeup has evolved. In the first movie, Katniss wears barely any makeup at all, but now she is more mature. "There are a couple of scenes where she's in her element in District Twelve, looking very fresh and simple and innocent," says makeup artist Ve Neill. "But for the most part she is wearing more makeup this time — her look is a lot different — because she is spending more time in front of the Capitol's cameras." When she attends the Capitol party, Katniss's makeup is bold and dominant, in keeping with the dress and the role she is playing: victor returning to the arena.

"You're absolutely terrifying me in that getup. What happened to the pretty little-girl dresses?" [Finnick] asks. . . . "I outgrew them," I say. — Catching Fire

The dark and attention-grabbing outfit Katniss (Jennifer Lawrence) wears for the parade is designed by Cinna (Lenny Kravitz).

KATNISS'S WEDDING DRESS

Trish Summerville knew that Katniss's wedding dress would need to be magnificent and one of a kind. She was looking for inspiration online when she happened to come across the work of designer Tex Saverio. He was based in Indonesia, but his reputation was growing in the United States. Lady Gaga had recently appeared on the cover of *Harper's Bazaar* in one of his dresses, and wore another of his avant-garde designs in her *Born This Way* Ball world tour. Kim Kardashian was also dressed in a design from his *La Glacon* collection for a high-fashion photo shoot in *Elle* magazine.

Summerville first reached out to Saverio via Skype, and "he literally did sketches right there," she says. At first, Summerville was intrigued by a black dress he'd done for a runway show, but when she saw his wedding dresses, she knew at once she'd found a designer for Katniss.

The dresses were from a collection Saverio called *La Glacon*, or "the ice cube."

"Just as an ice cube is at once fragile and strong," he explains, "so is the woman who will wear the clothes in this collection. Katniss, also, embodies these extremes. Strong and brave to replace her sister, but fragile in the face of the Capitol."

The upper part of the dress was made of metal, with a cage effect that Summerville loved. "But I wanted a different bottom on the dress," she recalls, "because Katniss has to twirl, and I needed the bottom of the dress to get a bit of height. A bit of air. And I wanted to have some feather pieces on it. Not literally feathers, but these laser cutouts that are almost like peacock feathers. So I think he ended up compiling three dresses together to give us our wedding dress."

ABOVE: TWO DRESSES FROM TEX SAVERIO'S *LA GLACON* COLLECTION THAT SERVED AS INSPIRATION FOR KATNISS'S WEDDING DRESS. RIGHT: KATNISS (JENNIFER LAWRENCE) POSES IN HER WEDDING DRESS DURING HER INTERVIEW WITH CAESAR FLICKERMAN (STANLEY TUCCI).

Saverio and his brother flew out for one of the first fittings with Jennifer Lawrence, and Summerville was surprised to see that the dress came in a gigantic crate. "It literally had its own stand on a dress form, and we had to put it in a truck to get it from Point A to Point B. When Jen did the photo session, we put her

on a little dolly, in the dress, then pulled her across the stage and into an elevator." With the skirt nearly five feet in circumference, it wasn't easy to maneuver, or simple to wear, but the dress was striking and utterly perfect.

Linda Flowers and Ve Neill put the finishing touches on Katniss's look for the scene. Flowers remembers: "When I saw the wedding dress, I had to take a minute and just quietly think about what I wanted to do for it, because the dress was so stunning. It was so elaborate that I knew I couldn't try to compete with it. Simple hair was the perfect complement to that dress."

Neill adds, "I gave her all this beautiful, silvery sparkly makeup, and I cut up some black feathered eyelashes. I put one black feather at the back end of both of her eyelashes, which gave her a sweeping kind of an eye. Then, when the dress burned off, she still had that feather on."

As victors, Haymitch Abernathy (Woody Harrelson) and Peeta Mellark (Josh Hutcherson) both wear clothing provided by the Capitol.

PEETA MELLARK

Like Katniss, Peeta has changed in some important ways since he's returned from the Hunger Games. He, too, has been traumatized by his time in the arena, and is trying to process all that happened to him there. "He's much more masculine and mature," says Trish Summerville. "He's been through a lot, he's grown a lot. There's been a transition since the last movie, and I wanted to find a way to show that through his clothes."

When Peeta goes to the Capitol, he wears suits instead of just shirts. His haircut seems more appropriate for a man than a boy. Summerville dressed him in leather pants, also, to show the way Peeta has made a break with his past. Summerville

No outfit is too extreme for a Capitol party. Katniss (Jennifer Lawrence), Effie (Elizabeth Banks), and Peeta (Josh Hutcherson).

Peeta (Josh Hutcherson) knows how to charm an audience during his interviews with Caesar Flickerman (Stanley Tucci).

smiles, saying, "He's great in leather pants. Once for the chariots, and then again for the party scene. I told Josh they'd be great for his motorcycle!"

Throughout the movie, Peeta's love for Katniss remains constant, and Summerville even found a way to work his feelings into his wardrobe. "I have Peeta wearing a lot of green because that's Katniss's favorite color," she says. "Subconsciously, he's always kind of wooing her." Later, when Katniss begins to warm up to him, she begins to wear his favorite color, too. Audiences might not notice these details at first, but they grow organically from the story.

CINNA

Though Cinna's designs take center stage in *The Hunger Games: Catching Fire*, the character himself is not particularly showy. Designer Trish Summerville wanted to respect that, and to dress actor Lenny Kravitz in a way that was cool and natural. "For the Capitol, he's not very outlandish or over-the-top. He's more like most stylists I know. . . . He needs to be able to step back and disappear. He never wants to be the center of attention. He's very demure and very deep, and he has this really strong connection with his tributes, so I kept him in dark tones. A little bit of burgundy, but a lot of blacks, some grays. And some signature pieces of jewelry."

Peeta (Josh Hutcherson)

FINNICK ODAIR

When Katniss first meets victor Finnick Odair in the novel *Catching Fire*, he is almost naked. The filmmakers needed to find a way to capture the tension of that moment from the book, while still remaining sensitive to the actor.

Trish Summerville recalls, "In the book it says he's just wearing a loincloth — gold with a little knot in front — but Sam was a little nervous about that. So we came up with the idea of having it be this gold net, because he's from the fishing district. It was more gladiator-like, where it could be a longer skirt, a wrapped piece. Then we gave him substantial boots underneath. His character is very masculine, but with a soft side to him.

"He was great to work with," Summerville continues. "The first couple of fittings he came in and didn't even look in the mirror. If I liked the way he looked, he liked it, too."

As she designed his costume for the interview with Caesar Flickerman, Summerville let it slip that, since he was from the fishing district, Finnick would be wearing an outfit made of fish. "I had ordered all these fish pelts — you can order them like leather. I think he thought I was a little bit crazy. But when we put the whole outfit together, Sam looked in the mirror and he said, 'I love my fish skirt!' That made me really happy because it was hard to get these guys to be open about wearing skirts at all."

As Finnick, Sam Claflin wore next to no

Finnick (Sam Claflin) offers Katniss a sugar cube.
Opposite: Finnick (Sam Claflin) is from the fishing district, and his outfit for his interview with Caesar Flickerman (Stanley Tucci) reflects that.

makeup. Ve Neill says, "All I had to do was give him a tan and make him glow, and Finnick came to life." Because the book called for him to have copper-colored hair, though, Claflin went through a color process to give his hair some glints of red. In addition, "I gave him that kind of tossed, messy look that separates him from the Capitol, where everyone is so groomed," says Linda Flowers.

EFFIE TRINKET

As in the first film, Effie Trinket's clothing reflects all of the excesses of the Capitol. Effie evolves as a character over the course of *The Hunger Games: Catching Fire*, as her initial pride in Katniss and Peeta is replaced by dismay when they go back into the arena. Her clothing, though, doesn't show much of her sensitive side. From beginning to end, she takes fashion to extremes. Over the course of the film, Effie has seven outrageously unique looks.

Trish Summerville looked to famously decadent and dramatic high-fashion designers to inform Effie's look. Summerville says, "There's this level of her that's really fun and bubbly, but there's

"There's this level of her that's really fun and bubbly, but there's also this part that suffers for fashion because that's how she deals with being a part of the Capitol. She's restricted and not really free to be who she is."
— Trish Summerville

also this part that suffers for fashion because that's how she deals with being a part of the Capitol. She's restricted and not really free to be who she is. My designs for Effie reflect both sides of her character. There's the cobalt-blue faux fur, with these crazy massive sleeves . . . that's the comic side. But Effie's clothes are also really uncomfortable, which speaks to the other side of her character, the part that can't get comfortable in the Capitol."

"Effie's my pet project," admits Linda Flowers. "She's one of my favorite characters of all time. Effie is like the Zsa Zsa [Gabor] of the Capitol. Everything is

TRISH SUMMERVILLE, COSTUME DESIGNER, WITH ELIZABETH BANKS (EFFIE).

Makeup artist Ve Neill applies the finishing touches to Elizabeth Banks's face.

overdone — her makeup, nails, shoes, hair, eyelashes. Everything is the most extreme, and then you put it all together and it looks amazing. She's over-the-top, but she has a heart, you know? She's just been sort of caught up in the wave of life in the Capitol." Elizabeth Banks adds, "Trish Summerville and her team are incredible. They used their own designs and also looked to some of the best designers in the world for their ideas of what's futuristic. Effie's bigger and better than ever. We're really exploring the flamboyance and amazingness that can be Capitol couture."

EFFIE TRINKET IN ONE OF HER MANY LOOKS.

Summerville says that it wouldn't have been possible to create Effie's look without the patience and good humor of actress Elizabeth Banks. "She's so great. She lets us torture her for a bit of fashion, just like Effie would, I think," Summerville says. Linda Flowers and Ve Neill also spent long hours with Banks, experimenting with different styles to get Effie's look just right. For example, Flowers knew she would have to create a golden wig for Effie to wear, but that was more difficult than it sounded. "Gold is a really hard color to achieve in hair, because it ends up looking blonde, and I knew it had to look gold. I spent two days just trying out different products to get the right color. Elizabeth is such a giving actress . . . she'd just sit in the chair, and we'd play."

THE AVOXES

Capitol fashion is constantly changing, even for the Avoxes — people who have been punished by the Capitol, had their tongues cut out, and are forced to work as servants. Makeup artist Ve Neill says, "They have these beautiful light-colored gowns on, with these cages around their faces. So I redesigned them to be completely white-faced, with a sort of ghoul makeup underneath. They have a very haunted and mysterious look about them."

The team behind Katniss and Peeta: Cinna (Lenny Kravitz), Haymitch (Woody Harrelson), and Effie (Elizabeth Banks)

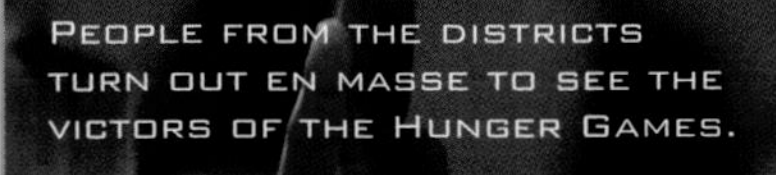
People from the districts turn out en masse to see the victors of the Hunger Games.

THE DISTRICTS

Even though Katniss and Peeta see little of each district on the Victory Tour, Summerville and her team developed unique looks for each region. The districts have hardly any communication with one another, and each serves a completely different purpose for the Capitol, so distinct fashions have sprung up organically in each place.

"Since we never saw the textile district in the first film," says Summerville, "I had the liberty of developing it myself. Their clothing is more vibrant than some of the other districts. It's not an ethnic

flair exactly, but a collision of many colors and textures. Different tapestries, different yarns."

In the fishing district — District 4, home to Finnick — she kept the clothes light and airy, in a blue-green palette that contrasted with the darker palette of, say, the coal district.

HAYMITCH ABERNATHY

Trish Summerville had fun dressing Haymitch. "He's a victor, so he gets his clothes from the Capitol, and they're chic and streamlined. We used textural fabrics to make garments that are modern, but with a relaxed feel. Still, there's always something kind of wrinkly about him, or his collar's not buttoned quite right. He's willing to wear these clothes, but he's got to do it on his own terms."

THE PRESIDENT'S PARTY

President Snow's party is one of the visual centerpieces of the movie, so the costume, hair, and makeup teams went all out with their planning for the celebration. In addition to outfitting the lead actors, they also created unique looks for some 300 extras. Planning and producing the party scenes required extraordinary cooperation and coordination among the different design teams.

Director Lawrence says, "We tried to imagine who the people would be within the Capitol, why they are invited to this party. There are people that are part of Snow's cabinet, people that are artists, people that are bankers and technicians . . . and they would all look and feel different. So once you take five hundred people and break them down into these categories, you can approach each one a little differently. Then within each category, there would be a range of looks, so each person had an individual style. And we had to figure out what unified them

"We tried to imagine who the people would be within the Capitol, why they are invited to this party. There would be a range of looks, so each person had an individual style."
— Francis Lawrence

within one pop cultural moment in the Capitol, so we did that with a certain color palette — pinks and blues and burgundies and fuchsias — as well as geometrical looks in the hair."

The cast of extras was chosen ahead of time and pre-fit in costumes, because there wouldn't be time to choose hundreds of costumes on the day of the

PRESIDENT SNOW (DONALD SUTHERLAND) STANDS ON HIS BALCONY, A SIGNATURE WHITE ROSE IN HIS BUTTONHOLE.

Effie Trinket (Elizabeth Banks), dressed for the party of the year.

shoot. "At some point, we were doing about a hundred and six fittings a day," Summerville recalls. "I'd pull the clothes after looking at the headshots, get all the options ready. I was working with six fitters and a whole tailor shop. Then we'd photograph the fittings and make charts to lay out the extras at the party, figure out where they should go." The photographs from the fittings would be used on the day of the actual shoot, so that the looks would be easy to replicate. They'd also go to the hair and makeup team.

Once they knew what the costumes were, Linda Flowers and Ve Neill created cohesive looks for hair and makeup. Flowers says, "When you have three hundred people, you have to have three hundred hairpieces, or three hundred plans, whether it's pre-cutting

PRESIDENT SNOW

Trish Summerville decided to give President Snow a military feel, while keeping in mind that this is Panem: His look is bound to be lush and fashionable, too. She says, "I was trying to make him a bit darker, a bit more buttoned-up, more totalitarian and in control this time, since the rebellions are starting to happen. He was really great about letting us tighten in his hair, bring his mustache out a bit more, give him darker, more saturated colors." Since there were winter scenes in the film, Summerville could contrast the military look with some faux fur and more decadent fabrics.

or pre-coloring or some kind of hair art. It took three weeks to get all the hair ready."

Even with careful advance planning, though, the day of the shoot was a massive undertaking. Flowers had forty hairstylists and ten interns on hand to create the looks she had designed. Neill and key makeup artist Nikoletta Skarlatos had twenty-five makeup artists from Los Angeles and another twenty from Atlanta. "We purposely pulled together an extraordinary group," Skarlatos says. "And when you have the best talent in the world in one room, only great things can happen. We just let them go to town."

In the Swan House, a giant ballroom was set up with some ninety makeup and hair stations. "We did lots of people with fabulous geometric patterns painted on their faces, some beautiful freehand work with beautiful design stencils," Ve Neill remembers. Skarlatos adds, "Somebody might have a strong eye and a really pale face, or a really strong lip and no eye whatsoever. Or just something really asymmetrical. Our objective was to create a unique look for each and every individual."

Together, these individual looks created an opulent party scene, at once spectacular and unsettling.

THE CAPITOL CROWD ENJOYS THE SPECTACLE OF THE PARADE.

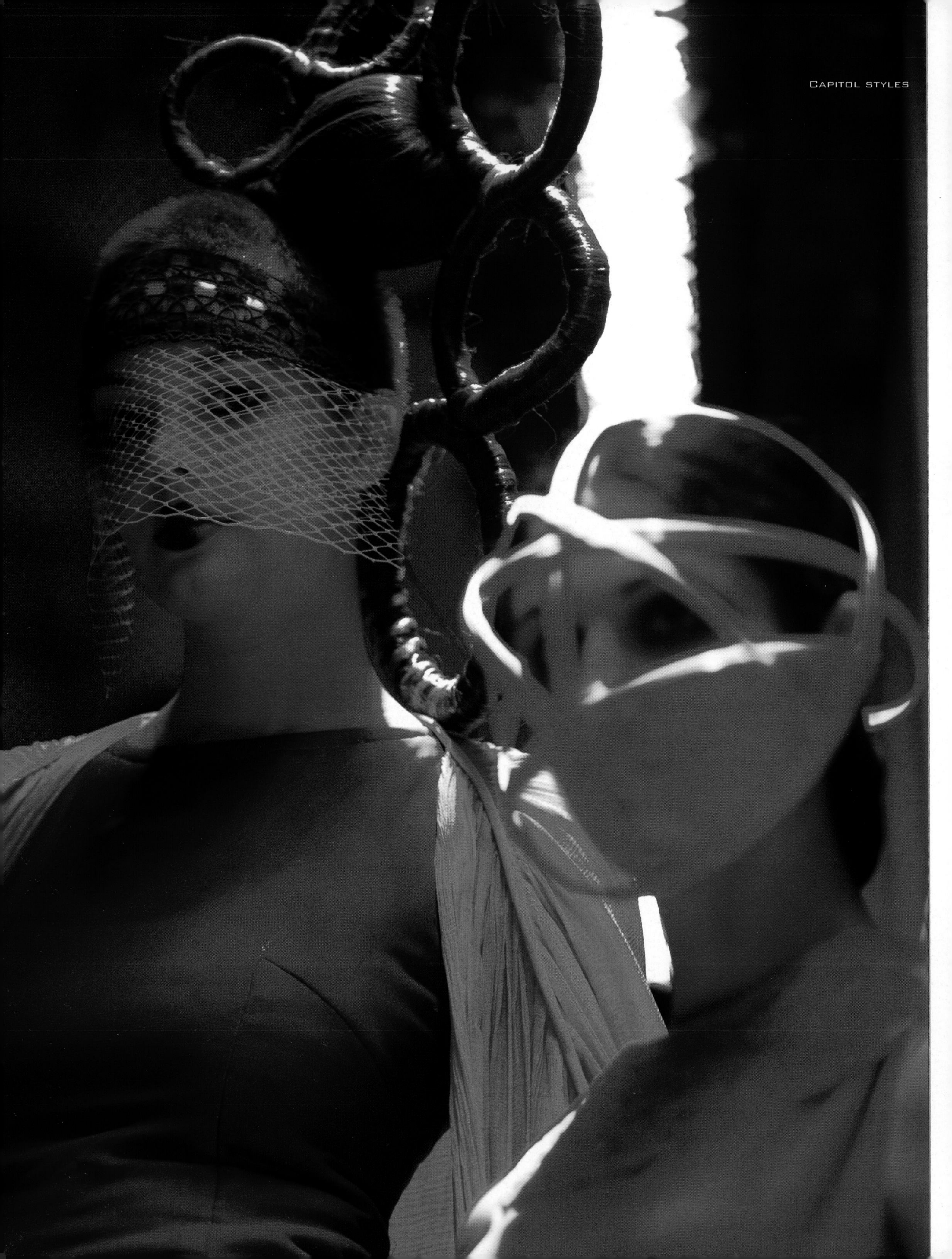

Katniss (Jennifer Lawrence) prepares for the chariot parade.

THE TRIBUTES' PARADE

The tributes' parade built on some of the districts' fashion, but presented new challenges. Trish Summerville says, "This sequence is tricky, because you're trying to do something that relates to the district they're from, but not all of the districts have themes that lend themselves to clothing. You don't want it to be too serious, because there's a bit of tongue-in-cheek to this parade, but it can be hard to come up with something clever."

For some districts, the key was to find materials that were unique to the region, and build around them. For other districts, the victors' costumes capture the mood or the attitude of the place.

For example, Brutus and Enobaria, the victors from District 2, are dressed to show their district's intimidating wealth and power. "Their costumes are hard and severe," explains Summerville. "The two of them are like gladiators."

The victors from District 4, the fishing district, have netlike material in their costumes, suggesting

Haymitch (Woody Harrelson) with Seeder (Maria Howell) and Chaff (E. Roger Mitchell), victors from District 11.

the fishing nets that are commonly used for industry where they live.

But Summerville took a slightly different approach with the victors from District 6, the transportation district. Their costumes don't reflect anything about transportation, but suggest the characters' addiction to a dangerous painkiller called morphling. Summerville says, "I kept them really dark, really goth, with camouflage patterns on their leathers that I then muted out." Like the gladiator costumes, the morphlings' costumes hinted at the roles they would play in the arena.

JOHANNA MASON

Makeup artist Nikoletta Skarlatos had worked with the actress playing Johanna Mason, Jena Malone, on two previous films, so she felt a great connection to her. She was excited to work on a look for this fierce and fearless character who feels she has nothing to lose. Skarlatos knew that the tributes from Johanna's lumber district always had to wear tree-themed costumes. Together with Trish Summerville, she pushed that look to the next level. "Trish designed this amazing outfit that had an element of real cork in it, and I used the makeup to create these tree branches coming out of her eyes for the chariot scene, which was really quite scary. Her makeup in general gives her a kind of fearless look."

Cinna (Lenny Kravitz) takes one last moment with Katniss (Jennifer Lawrence)

UNIFORMS FOR THE GAMES

Because they wear them throughout the Quarter Quell, the victors' costumes are important elements of the Games. They need to look attractive enough to capture the interest of viewers in the Capitol, while still being practical enough for tributes to wear in whatever situations the Gamemakers create for them.

Trish Summerville remembers, "In the book it says they're in sheer blue jumpsuits, but that was one thing that didn't really translate into film, or work functionally. The actors were worried about what they'd wear underneath. So we had a big discussion with Francis and Nina, and then they discussed with Suzanne what kind of flexibility we might have. We needed something the tributes could do stunts in, that they could wear for a long time, that would look flattering on a range of body types. I started with an illustrator and I started doing sketches of things that could work in water and on land. We also needed to figure out the fabrication of the garments, what would keep [the actors] warm while they were underwater."

ENOBARIA (META GOLDING) AND BRUTUS (BRUNO GUNN) SCRAMBLE THROUGH THE JUNGLE.

Katniss (Jennifer Lawrence) helps Wiress (Amanda Plummer) recover after the blood rain.

Ultimately, Summerville and her team decided on a black suit, with gray and metallic elements that would pop in the jungle scenes. "We did three-dimensional grid paintings on the front and sides to give the suits more shape," she explains. "Our goal was to develop something flattering and functional that would look good on camera." The lead characters had several variations of the suit, also, to allow for different stunts.

> **"We needed something the tributes could do stunts in, that they could wear for a long time, that would look flattering on a range of body types . . . that could work in water and on land."**
> **— Trish Summerville**

Inside the arena, hair and makeup were less dramatic. Ve Neill says, "It's almost impossible to keep anything on anybody's face when they're wet and sweaty, when they're covered in cuts and bruises." Instead, she gave the characters deep tans, like most people would have if they were outside for days on end. "We didn't want them to go out and get sun damage, mind you," Neill says. "So we used tanning products. Whatever we could do so they wouldn't have to wear a foundation."

Like many of the Capitol's affectations, fashion and makeup are stripped away when the victors enter the arena, and their focus turns to only one matter: staying alive. Once the Quarter Quell begins, the attention of the Capitol audience shifts away from fashion and to the action of the Games.

PLUTARCH HEAVENSBEE

Head Gamemaker Plutarch Heavensbee was an interesting character to dress. Trish Summerville muses that "he has this duality to him, where he's pretending to be one thing and another thing comes through later." His costumes reflect that. "We tried not to make him too over-the-top, like the other people in the Capitol," she says. "We kept his lines simple, modern. His colors are always kind of open because he's this sarcastic, relaxed kind of guy. He's assured of who he is and what he's doing, enough that he can even challenge Snow."

PART 6

LOOKING AHEAD

THE SPARK

All it takes is one spark to start a fire. And once it's started, a fire can be unstoppable. As long as it has enough fuel, it will burn ever hotter and brighter until it is extinguished.

Katniss's desperate choice at the end of *The Hunger Games* is the spark that rouses Panem. The country's miserable conditions are just right for the revolutionary flames to spread.

By the end of *The Hunger Games: Catching Fire*, Katniss's one brave act has caused an inferno. The flames are growing ever closer to President Snow, and in spite of his best efforts — in spite of creating an arena designed to crush the spirits of the districts — he has failed to put them out.

So what's next? Destruction. Revolution. War.

Every member of *The Hunger Games: Catching Fire*'s team knows that the next part of Katniss's story will grow from the tension and shock at the end of this one. Things will grow darker and more difficult for Katniss until the smoke begins to clear.

> ***The bird, the pin, the song, the berries, the watch, the cracker, the dress that burst into flames. I am the mockingjay.***
> ***— Catching Fire***

Elizabeth Banks says, "If we're talking about *The Hunger Games* as a superhero movie, *The Hunger Games* introduces Katniss. It's the origin story. Who is she, where does she come from, how does she affect people? Then *The Hunger Games: Catching Fire* . . . it's just what the title says. Katniss is a burning ember that eventually burns the doors off the place. Now the idea of revolution is spreading, and in *Mockingjay* the Capitol will really feel the wrath of the districts."

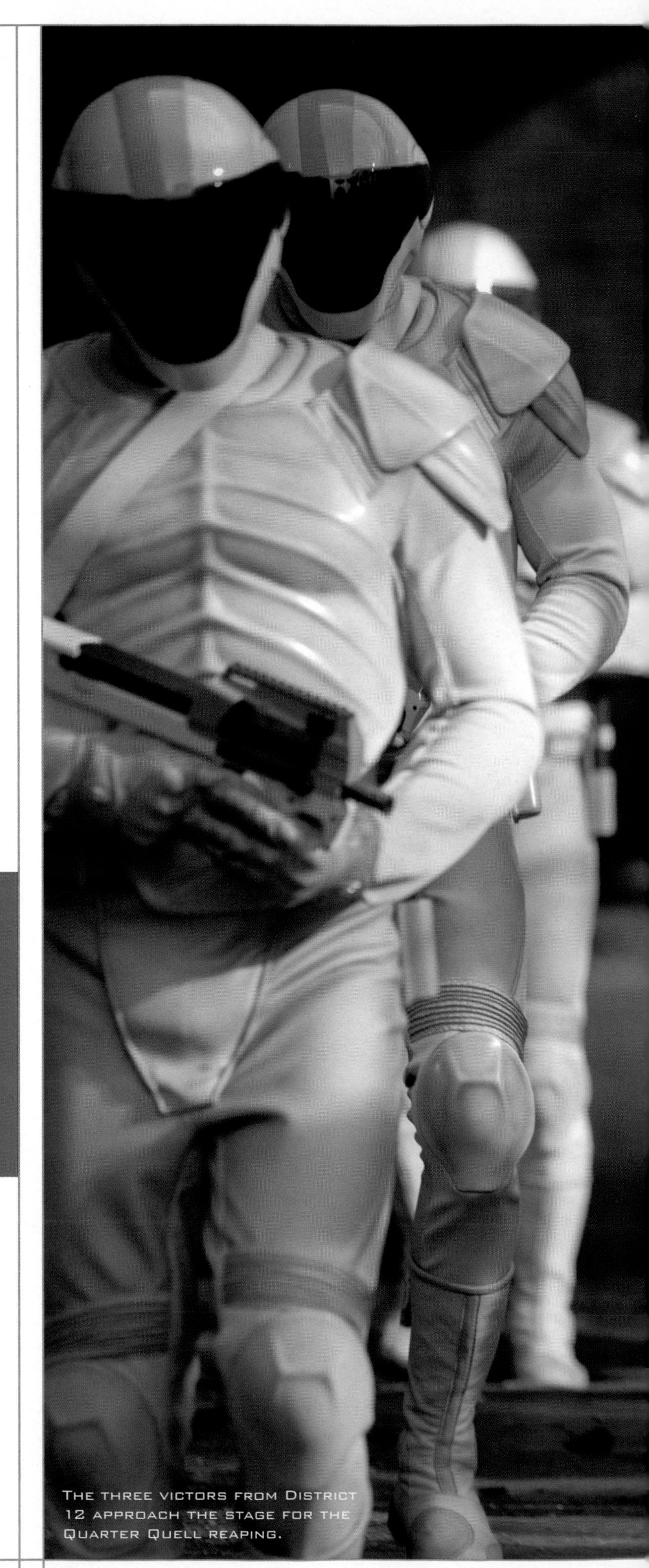

THE THREE VICTORS FROM DISTRICT 12 APPROACH THE STAGE FOR THE QUARTER QUELL REAPING.

Josh Hutcherson adds, "The uprising has begun, and we're starting to see the moving parts come together to overthrow a government. It's kind of amazing, I think, to see Katniss go through her struggle to rise to the heroic status Panem needs. When you can make the world a better place, you feel an obligation to do that, and that's one thing that Katniss comes to realize."

Jennifer Lawrence sees parallels between the character of Katniss and another strong female figure, from centuries ago. "This is an incredible story about a girl that doesn't want to be a hero, but finds

KATNISS (JENNIFER LAWRENCE) TAKES AIM.

herself in a position where she is forced to be, and turns into a futuristic Joan of Arc," she says.

The next films, will show the many facets of the revolution, from the triumphant to the tragic. Katniss will struggle with her role in the rebellion, and with its effects on the people she loves the most.

She's growing as a character, the scope of her awareness ever increasing. As Lionsgate's Erik Feig says, "In the arc of the trilogy, Katniss's circle of caring gets broader in a highly realistic and relatable way. In the beginning of *The Hunger Games*, she mostly cares about herself and about Prim. In *Catching Fire*, she starts to see that she also cares about Peeta and she cares about Gale, then maybe by the end she cares about some of the tributes as well. Then, in *Mockingjay*, we see that she cares about her family, she cares about the larger group, and ultimately she begins to care about the citizens of Panem. Her growth mirrors the growth that we all go through, from being true individuals to becoming part of a civic community."

"This is an incredible story about a girl that doesn't want to be a hero, but finds herself in a position where she is forced to be." — Jennifer Lawrence

Jeffrey Wright, who plays Beetee in this film, puts it like this: "I think there's an examination here, particularly as the story advances and we get past *The Hunger Games: Catching Fire*, of the price that warriors pay for the work that they do." Katniss must consider whether war is worthwhile, given the terrible toll it takes on the people who fight it and the people who are caught in the cross fire.

These are weighty questions for a franchise with a huge teen audience, but author Suzanne Collins has never flinched from addressing the subject of war in any of her books for readers of all ages.

Violence is an essential element of telling a war story, and director Lawrence is careful to keep it to a manageable level in the film. For one thing, he does not want to do with his movie what the Capitol

Katniss (Jennifer Lawrence)

does with its Games: glamorize violence and desensitize viewers to its pain.

While the violence is important for communicating Collins's ideas about war, the story is ultimately not about the firestorm that rages around Katniss. It is about Katniss herself, and the way these events change her life forever. Francis Lawrence says, "Katniss's need for survival, her need to protect the people she loves, both feel very natural to any of us. You see her on-screen, and you can transplant yourself into her situation — I think that's one reason she is such a memorable character."

Over the course of the trilogy, she goes from being a tribute to a rebel, then from a rebel to the face of a war. At the end of *The Hunger Games: Catching Fire*, she is only partly down this path. Producer Nina Jacobson explains, "Katniss doesn't yet see herself as a leader, but she is slowly growing into the role she assumes in the third book."

"Katniss's need for survival, her need to protect the people she loves, both feel very natural to any of us." — Francis Lawrence

The Hunger Games: Catching Fire takes Katniss halfway there, and its shocking ending will leave audiences hungry for more *Hunger Games*. The movie offers an irresistible combination of superlative acting and superlative characters, or, as Erik Feig puts it, "We have one of the era's greatest actresses and one of the era's best literary creations in a film by a brilliant visual stylist who also has an intense emotional connection to the material."

The Hunger Games: Catching Fire is the next chapter in this epic story, one of the most compelling films of the twenty-first century so far.